NIGHT

THE PEGASUS PRIZE FOR LITERATURE

NIGHT

A NOVEL BY

BILGÉ KARASU

Translated by Güneli Gün,

with the author

LOUISIANA STATE UNIVERSITY PRESS / BATON ROUGE AND LONDON / 1994

Copyright ©1985 by Bilgé Karasu
Copyright © 1991 by Metis Yayınları, Istanbul
Translation copyright © 1994 by Louisiana State University Press
Originally published as *Gece* by İletişim Yayınları, Istanbul
Manufactured in the United States of America
First printing
03 02 01 00 99 98 97 96 95 94   5 4 3 2 1

Designer: Amanda McDonald Key
Typeface: Bembo
Typesetter: G&S Typesetters, Inc.
Printer and binder: Thomson-Shore, Inc.

LIBRARY OF CONGRESS CATALOGING-IN-PUBLICATION DATA

Karasu, Bilge
    [Gece. English]
    Night : a novel / by Bilgé Karasu ; translated by Güneli Gün,
      with the author.
        p.   cm. — (Pegasus Prize for Literature)
    ISBN 0-8071-1849-4
    I. Title. II. Series.
    PL248.K33G4313   1994
    894'.3533—dc20   93-37912
                                                                CIP

The paper in this book meets the guidelines for permanence and durability of
the Committee on Production Guidelines for Book Longevity of the Council
on Library Resources. ∞

Publisher's Note

The Pegasus Prize for Literature was established by Mobil Corporation to introduce American readers to distinguished works from countries whose literature is rarely translated into English. *Night,* by Bilgé Karasu, was awarded the Pegasus Prize in Istanbul in November, 1991, after an independent jury selected it from among the best novels written in Turkey in the preceding ten years. The novel, which first appeared in Turkey in 1984, is part of a body of work by the author that includes novels, short-story collections, and experimental written forms Mr. Karasu calls "texts." In 1971, Mr. Karasu won the Sait Faik Short Story Award, having won the Turkish Language Society's Translation Award in 1963. He is at present a lecturer in philosophy at Hacettepe University, in Ankara.

The honorary chairman of the Turkish jury was Professor Talat Sait Halman, chairman of New York University's Department of Near Eastern Languages and Literature, and formerly Turkish minister of culture. Other jury members were Hulki Aktunç, a journalist and critic; Necla Aytür, professor of American Literature at Ankara University; Doğan Hızlan, a literary critic with Istanbul's *Hürriyet* daily; Ahmet Oktay, a poet, writer, and critic with *Milliyet;* Selim Ileri, a poet and editor; and Tahsin Yücel, a novelist, critic, and professor at the University of Istanbul.

Night, like most of Mr. Karasu's fiction, seeks to break the barriers of traditional narrative by constructing a "new reality," in the words of the late Jonathan Kistler. Resident in an unnamed city in a country that could be one of dozens, the narrator drifts above a "formless mass of dream"—in the epigraph the author draws from Jean Genet. Yet characters and plot eventually emerge . . . the narrator, victim of a surreal and Kafkaesque persecution at the hands of a vague and sinister agency; N, the head of that agency, and the narrator's rival since childhood; and Sevinç, a representative of the agency who for a time becomes the narrator's lover. Adding to the air of dream and nightmare in the work is the continual intervention of the writer, through footnotes that question the very credibility of what he is creating.

The daunting task of producing a translation of this novel—a translation subsequently revised by Mr. Karasu—fell to Güneli Gün, a Turkish-American novelist and translator, who has taught creative writing and translation workshops at Oberlin College. Ms. Gün's most recent novel, *On the Road to Baghdad*, appeared in 1991, and she has recently completed translating Orhan Pamuk's *The Black Book* for Farrar, Straus & Giroux.

On behalf of the author, we wish to express our appreciation to Mobil Corporation, which established the Pegasus Prize and provided for the translation of this volume into English.

To F. Akatlı

This translated edition to my friends T. and F. Stark. We shared so much.

every monday carries the seed of defeat
      —Turgut Uyar, "The Diary of Defeat," in *Every Monday*

Often at night I lie awake. I am the sentry guarding the sleep of others, whose master I am. I am the spirit floating above the formless mass of dream.

   . . . and they disappeared into a night distant, dangerous as all nights are.

   . . . he bore the dark sense of symbol and was dangerous as are all inhabitants of the night, all inhabitants of dreams. Dreams are peopled with characters, animals, plants, objects, which are all symbols. Each is powerful in itself, and when the one who has given rise to it takes the place of the symbol, he takes on this mysterious power. The power of the sign is the power of the dream.

      —Jean Genet, *Miracle of the Rose*

The movement of self-building individuality is . . . the becoming of the real world.

      —Hegel, *The Phenomenology of the Spirit*

I

1

Night slowly comes on. Descends. Already it has begun filling the hollows. Once these are full and it empties onto the plain, everything will turn gray. For a while no light will go on, in the hollows or out beyond. The glow on the hills will seem for a time to suffice; then the hills too will sink into darkness.

In this dark, the tongue alone will appear able to survive. In this place where no weight or reality remains. The one reality the darkness will seem to offer is in lending itself to being spoken. Between two people. Two walls.

Then clothes will start to come off, so that the night-inflicted wounds may smart all the more.

Firm young muscles will move into the night.

Flabby muscles will turn to jelly during the night.

Only the tongue will tell of the lights on the hills and in the underground palaces. Only language will speak of the single-celled creatures bathing in this light.

It is slowly getting dark. Up from our bowels night rises, up toward the heart and the eyes.

2

It is early afternoon when the first nightworkers appear in the streets. Even if only a few.

Their job is to get night ready: by digging holes, for example, where night may easily collect when it comes.

Their job is to prepare people for the night: to take young muscles and get them used to stripping down for when the night will require that. To get them used to the longest night by penetrating their naked flesh with cold, thin metal rods or by burying red-hot buckshot within it.

By evening the nightworkers become easy for everybody to spot. Tools in hand, they wander through the streets in ever-increasing numbers, preparing the night, preparing for the night.

The tools they bear are fashioned of iron, cut from well-tanned hides, carved from choice timber, or molded from pliant resins. They serve to pound, tear, pierce, gouge, twist, and snap off. Also to burn and to break.

These tools have been designed and specially made for use on young bodies.

3

The nightworkers have been around since early afternoon, although few people have noticed them.

It is rumored that nightworkers like square loaves of bread. They may not be the only ones in this great city who like square bread. But the bakers, tobacconists, and grocers think that all who ask for square bread must somehow be nightworkers.

In shops where bread is sold, round, long, and rectangular loaves of bread are also available. In midafternoon, when children return from school, business begins to pick up. More and more loaves are sold—round, rectangular, long, oval, square. Hands—small, large, bony, soft, dirty, clean, callused, sticky— carry them off.

The nightworkers walk the alleys, watching into which houses the round, rectangular, oval, and long loaves make their way. Although they proceed rather casually, those who observe carefully will from time to time see one of them go up to a door and put an unobtrusive mark on it somewhere or other. The keen observer is puzzled. In the houses so marked, square bread is never eaten, yet the marks give no clue as to the shape of the loaves consumed. Indeed, the doors have been marked somewhat at random. Or, at least, so it seems.

4

On one of the hills—not the highest nor the most prominent but the one next to it—lives the Corrector in his solitude. In silence.

The Corrector's solitude is not to be underestimated, especially after nightfall. From his window, he has watched the night pour down on the earth, first into the hollows, especially those dug by the nightworkers, then spread over the plain. He has followed it moment by moment. He has seen light fade from the face of the earth and has glanced at the windows of the houses, still dark.

He has not wanted to accept the impossibility of keeping night from gnawing at the day. He has thought at length of how to thwart the nightworkers, how to keep the light from going out on the earth.

A person may not want to believe that something is impossible but may go on living anyway, without being torn apart, when forced to accept that it is. If, in fact, the Corrector's solitude becomes increasingly bitter as each surface on the earth is plunged into darkness, it's because he finds himself helpless before a problem he has for so long pondered and been unable to solve.

For the moment the only entity that appears to have been able to survive in the dark, as we have said, is language. The tongue . . . knows the Corrector's solitude and speaks of it.

Or rather, for the time being, it is able to speak. Once darkness falls, covering everything including the tongue, nothing but hoot owls will fly through the night, nothing but bats. Nothing but their screech and rustle will be heard. Then the Corrector's solitude will close in on him like the walls of a well.

Owls, bats, the night-fed, the day-blind.

5

Tongues begin to awaken, first of all, to get untied . . .

For a long time they have held back the things they would say, but now that they have broken loose, they will say anything.

They speak on several levels.

On the lowest level, for instance, they say, Why do night-workers wear such peculiar headgear?

But if there is a pair of eyes above the tongue that can still take in the world, what they say will be somewhat different.

This headgear has always been around, but it has gone through minute, almost undetectable changes to reach its present form. The back has reached down to cover all the hair and half the neck as well. (And since they have been wearing their collars higher and higher, the workers no longer appear to have necks at all.) Then the sides grew until only the earlobes remained exposed, while the front finally came down over the eyes so as to hide them. Meanwhile, the workers have grown moustaches and beards.

With headgear obliterating half the face, and a moustache and beard hiding the rest, each nightworker looks like every other. Without the headgear and the moustaches and beards, none would be recognized by their fellow nightworkers. Their parents wouldn't recognize them, though, as they are now. What they want is to remain unrecognized, and to inspire in people nothing but awe for their terrible work.

6

The nightworkers had at first only hoped that by coming out early in the afternoon they would cause fear, but now they explore the different methods of diffusing and prolonging the fear they know they can inspire. They increase and diminish it at will, to intensify it. Observing the many ways people on the street and in the houses quail upon seeing them, the nightworkers seek further variations in the pleasure they find in others' terror. They are constantly trying to develop new methods. But when they go out in the afternoon, they sometimes surprise even themselves with what refinement they can discover in just a few hours.

This became clear to many people in the case of the young man they caught on one of the widest side streets off the city's main thoroughfare. What was done to him had all the freshness of inspired improvisation and the disconcerting simplicity of a master hand.

And that very same day, just after dark, they were to think of a more refined torment and, bemused, to regret that it had not occurred to them before.

Their new idea was in fact simple enough. All they had to do was just not move, and keep quiet. Nothing more. Stay out of sight, keep quiet, and act as if they were not there. For a few hours.

Hidden in their dark corners, they watched the troubled faces at the lighted windows, eyes furtively glancing left and right and then disappearing behind the curtains, hands darting out to whisk children off the streets. Men and women still out in the dark gazed straight ahead as they scurried home. The nightworkers' jackal ears picked up the sound of bolts easing into place. Their eyes followed the lights as they went out one by one. They experienced in every part of their flesh the ineffable pleasure that came from sensing the anxiety that gnawed the gut of people waiting for something ineluctable that did not occur.

7

FOOTNOTE 1. It's hard to affirm this, but some writers attain the greatest refinement of expression through words shot out like arrows, one after the other; others attain it through words flowing like underground waters. My language must strive for the suppleness and rhythm of a body bending and rising as it gathers flowers.

8

Everyone was upset by the incident on Fish Market Street, but no one was surprised.

Nobody knows why the nightworkers attacked the young man at the busiest hour on one of the widest streets leading into the main avenue, just a few feet off Grocer Street.

Some say that the bread he was carrying wasn't square; others, that his hair was not black; still others, that he walked with a limp. All these are rumors, of course. Nobody knows the truth. Indeed, is there even a truth to be known? No one's certain about even that. All that is known, or was seen, is that the workers suddenly converged from the walls, corners, and doorways to seize the young man from the crowd and surround him. When the workers melted away, they left behind only a lump of bleeding flesh. According to those who saw the winsome young man before losing sight of him in the mob of nightworkers, the lump left behind couldn't have constituted even half of his bulk. They sprinkled sawdust on the bloody mess and covered it with dry leaves.

Those who passed by the next morning saw in the dull, struggling daylight only a dusky stain on the pavement where the youth had been torn apart.

Now people peer at one another expecting to see clawlike hands and chop-licking tongues. But the workers, being nightworkers, don't appear in the morning light. Were these workers once like everybody else? There are those who'd like to believe they were.

Would that make them feel less terrified?

9

In the present situation, people like to believe whatever is less terrifying. Perhaps what I've called the Solitude of the Creator is something I want to believe in, something I believe in because I want to.

Perhaps the Creator—or the Corrector—does not feel alone at all as night now spreads slowly over the plain. Who knows? Although he seems to wish to resist the dimming of the light, it may be that he desires no such thing, and makes no effort to that end. By doing nothing, he may be encouraging the night-workers. In preparing the night, they may even be receiving assistance from the Author—not Corrector, not Creator, but Author.

Perhaps they set about their work with the hidden approval in the Author's heart as their accomplice.

Who can tell? Who is in a position to know except the Author himself and a few of his closest associates?

Yet, is the idea inconceivable? This is where what we said above becomes relevant: even if you did think of such a thing, you would say the idea was absurd and refuse to believe that it was possible.

People are increasingly satisfied to believe whatever they want to, or whatever they wish for; perhaps they are scarcely aware that they've left off reasoning, reflecting, attempting to see things as they really are. By the time they become aware, darkness will have set in. Even though the sun seems to rise each morning and light up the world, the darkness of night will never be altogether dispelled.

10

FOOTNOTE 2. Am I dragging things out, beating about the bush? So far, nothing much has occurred. Are the abruptness and the surprise of the transition something I really want? Yet, so far, I've been able to hint at only one of the themes I have in mind. Time to pull it all together, to decide whether the author of all this is me or one of my creations.

11

No matter how hard I tried, I couldn't recall setting down my briefcase, or keeping it open in the presence of others. Yet inside it I found papers I'd never seen before, although I had expected this and waited for it and deemed it inevitable. Folded. Unfamiliar in their whiteness. I unfolded them in the briefcase and hesitantly pushed aside the one on top. "——nemas and theaters are out of bounds. Within the next 24 hours, Sevinç may arrive." That seemed clear enough. Or was it?

Was Sevinç the name of the woman, perhaps, who took me to that tiny, dark registry room at the Ministry of Trials? Why should the possibility of such a coincidence not come to mind?

Narrow, dusty file rooms must be pretty much the same the world over. Books and movies have made that abundantly clear, have they not? Enlightened as we are, we have to be pleased that the one and only way of increasing efficiency is being adopted in our country too: as registry offices get ever smaller and stuffier, more and more people are seated at desks like sheep out to graze, the spaces between the desks are reduced to keep them from moving about, and in order to cut costs two people are assigned to sit opposite each other at the same desk.

Faced with what ought to terrify us, we act as if it's something auspicious; we do our best to content ourselves with what we're conceded. With such a basis for happiness, why should we choose to live in fear?

This morning the woman, whose name may have been Sevinç, came by my house to pick me up, and told me I had to go somewhere with her. I tried not to be scared; refusing to go never occurred to me. It was only after the car she had waiting out front began to speed along that I thought to ask, "Who are you?"

"It's of no consequence who I am," she said. "I'm only a messenger."

12

Daytime troubles the nightworkers. Darkness that stands behind the day, in their estimation, is a happiness that is absolute. For them, the land of Felicity exists only in a fairy-tale past where, once upon a time, this thickly shaded garden swaddled them, girded and fed them. They carry tirelessly the memory of a calm darkness that slipped from them as the day began to break—never to be retrieved. Within this calm, this twilight, they dream of a limitless ego embracing the universe, of galloping horses, of enemies vanquished, and of angers appeased only by the flow of blood. Not letting anything else survive.

When, somewhere in the night, the nightworkers dive into the dim waters of a dream and begin to swim, they are like adults carried back, borne by loving hands, to their childhood home. They are like the people who when looking out the window of that house, instead of the city they know and remember, can only see an unbounded spread of red earth . . . There where stood the familiar playgrounds, barracks, gardens, and parks they see now, as the only trace of the existence, the passage, of other people (the expression "other people" has an ambiguity with them: it means someone other than the self; it also means others than those they consider their equals or those they see as reflections of themselves), a stone barrier, for example, barely perceptible on the red earth. The meaningless, functionless stone barrier traverses the field of red soil from one end to the other. The dreamer perceives it slowly. The emptiness that this barrier (no matter how hard one looks, the huge equestrian statue that had once stood on an imposing stone dome at the center of the barrier is no longer visible) seems to cross, from one end to the other, is unbelievably vast; what meets the eye is like land that has been plowed and planted and has turned boggy after the first rains, yet not a single tree, beast, or human being can be detected. The earth is somewhere between orange and red, the stone barrier dirty white. Even the sky has turned the red of dawn or sunset, from reflecting the vast emptiness. This is the light of the hour when the day gives up the ghost, or when its hour of victory is still far off. Beyond this imponderable spread of land—only in dreams can such a "beyond" present itself— there are stains that resemble, perhaps, clumps of green, and shedlike shapes seem scattered around in clusters. But here there are no streets, no people. This is a city. But a city where no one but the observer exists. It is the shadow of a city, where even farming has been forgotten, a city dead, scraped off the face of the earth.

(For horses to gallop on this land, the vestiges of man have to be still further erased from the earth and the sky.)

Happiness for the nightworkers consists in seeing themselves on horses galloping, or watching the horses gallop in the middle of this land as the day sinks . . . but without leaving their window, the darkness of their window. It consists in believing it possible to suck an inexhaustible dark milk from a breast that never goes dry and to go on with a life of swimming, of flying, without waking up from the dream, without being denied the paradise that they don't want to believe is lost.

13

My briefcase was under my arm the whole time. Once we entered through the small, narrow back door, we embarked on endless passages. Getting there must have taken an hour. The streets and houses I saw from the car window were places I already knew, but it was also as if I were seeing them for the first time. I hadn't been out that way for years. How the city had grown and changed!

The woman beside me, as if weary of walking the passages, suddenly opened a door when I least expected it (just when she'd taken a step beyond it), and she pulled me inside. She sat me down at a table.

My briefcase was under my arm the whole time. A bald man, who wore no beard, no moustache, no glasses, and had neither eyebrows nor eyelashes, sat across from me—in a registry room where the dossiers went up like soft walls preparing to envelop and constrict us—and he began putting questions to me that, far from being strange, were just what I expected. Age, place of birth, year of birth, mother's name, father's name, occupation. Do you have any idea why we brought you here? You can't think of any reason? Did you leave town recently? (It's been years since I've been out of town.)

I don't know if my answers pleased them or not. When they were through with their questions, they stared at me long and hard. Then they exchanged glances. The man with no hair, no eyebrows nor eyelashes, rose from his seat as if to go to another room to get something, or as if suddenly having to pee, and went out the door. He never came back. The woman beside me kept looking at her watch, giving the impression of timing something. "All right," she said, "let's go." In seconds we were out on the street. At the door, she said, "Good-bye." I returned home. I opened my briefcase: "Within the next 24 hours, Sevinç . . ."

14

There exists a squad of nightworkers who do not carry chains, clubs, whips, or ropes. Tucked in the armpit, their only weapon is the stiletto, long and thin as a skewer; they don't so much carry the stiletto as make it part of their bodies. Or so one comes to believe, seeing them fold their arms and softly stroke their armpits.

They rarely use the stiletto. Their real job lies in other things. If they happen to be bothered in their work, they prefer other, natural, methods for getting rid of those who trouble them.

The assignment of this squad of nightworkers is to write on walls, doors, posts, roads, on every available surface whether of wood or stone. While people sleep or, having put out the lights, pass anxious hours in the dark, the squad goes all over the city, writing everywhere, Night Will Come. On small mornings following small nights, people come out on the streets only to read inscriptions heralding the approach of the big night, which will lead to no morning, not even the smallest. The inscriptions are sometimes abbreviated, occasionally reduced to single letters. It is known that on the following small night a bunch of hands will transform these letters into strange flowers and wild words, disguising them. And on the night after that, another small night, others carrying paintbrushes and paint will be out looking for a vacant spot on the walls, doors, stones, or roads. The thing is to avoid confrontation between the nightworkers and the bunch of hands. Otherwise the hands will turn into bleeding flowers on the walls and the streets. Rain and soapy water will in time wash away the blood, but they are ineffectual against paint.

15

I'd set out for a familiar house on a familiar street in a familiar neighborhood. Footsteps had so heavily pounded the snow that it was on the verge of turning to ice. I was cold. To get to my friend's house, I had to climb uphill for quite a while, then turn into a short, narrow side street, then into another narrow street that was parallel to the street on which I had started. To make it easier, I could go through an old house at the upper end of the street, out the back door into the yard, and to the street where my friend lived. Considering the bitter cold, I was disinclined to wind my way from street to street and decided to take the seeming shortcut; although I generally try not to go where I have no business, I put aside my scruples and ducked into the house. Children who had come in out of the cold were swarming under the staircase; they played so noisily that the whole house shook. A stone wall had been put up to block the way to the back door. I began to say, "The back door . . ." The children didn't wait for me to finish but aimed shouts in my direction. I understood that I had to go upstairs and then take the back stairs down. "They divided the house in two," said one of the bigger children. I started up the stairs, which seemed to get narrower and narrower. Mattresses and quilts were out on the landings, arranged in the way women who live in small houses pile them during spring cleaning. But spring cleaning in the middle of winter? It was months till spring. The children, who had followed me up the stairs, were again yelling, though at first I couldn't make out their words. They started pawing at me, hanging on to my pants and coattails. I had a hard time making my way down again to the front door. I'd given up on the shortcut. I was ready to go around on the street. Then came the voices of their mothers who'd stepped out their doors upstairs. I felt pursued. Suddenly I understood what they were all saying. They shouted in unison now, as if repeating some sort of jingle. "Daymaker," they said. "Daaaymaaaker!"

16

Much whispering has always gone around about who—or who all—the nightworkers have to obey. At first everyone put in his two cents' worth concerning the master's identity. Then three or four different names came to the fore. For a while everyone agreed on a name, but the agreement soon yielded to claims for another, or others, of the person or persons behind the bearer of the name first favored. Discussion went round and round. There are those who say that by watching the nightworkers operate, anyone can easily tell that they are loyal to a single man. It's only lately that these rumors have figured in much open debate. No one knows for sure the master's identity, but there's a lot of uninformed speculation concerning the person— or persons—the Man is thought to be. No one stands out, though, for the strength of his convictions on the question or for the certainty that what he says is true.

Still, it seems as if there's something everyone knows, something every mouth repeats: the Man, whoever he may be, inspires great loyalty, as well as great fear and caution, because he passes the same sentence on every offense committed, major or minor.

The sentence: death.

They say the Man believes that each nightworker has to be accustomed to killing human beings; any time a criminal must be put to death, he appoints the worker whose turn it is to do the job, according to the alphabetical order of the roster. That's what they say. Some people think that preparing the killers to consider that they too can be killed one day is a commendable policy that prevents their getting the least bit out of line. It's only lately that people have started saying that publicly. But those who don't want to believe such things, those who aren't so inclined, are in the majority. That is why hardly anyone comes straight out and denounces the Man, whoever he may be.

17

I somehow managed to bolt into the street, stricken with the mixture of anxiety, fear, and distress usually experienced only in the worst nightmares. The young and old were all shouting after me: "DAYMAKER! DAYMAKER!" I decided it was a new term of abuse. But I couldn't recall this particular insult from the writing the nightworkers left on walls and stones. I still don't recall having seen it anywhere. This morning I checked out the roads and the posts again. No such word anywhere. Yet that day there was something aggressively insulting in the children's shouts. *Daymaker* might be used in opposition to *nightmaker*. But I am possibly the only person for whom *nightmaker* has a developed meaning. Or do I have the impression of being the first to come up with or discover something that was common knowledge?

That day I turned off into the side street but didn't venture to my friend's house. Right then I was tempted to say, I never want to set foot in this neighborhood again. Instead, I said, I'll wait, and one day, if I lose this fear . . .

I didn't phone my friend, either. Who knows? Those who shouted after me that way might well have made it impossible for him to go on living in the neighborhood. Yet he and I had always thought we didn't do things to disturb or offend people.

At the very worst, I might be described as someone who doesn't know the value of friendship, or of a friend, since I didn't visit my friend that day or look him up after that.

But that isn't quite right either. I'm not being honest. What I said might be true up to the point where I turned off and reached the corner of the street my friend lives on. But when I arrived at the corner . . .

18

If the great, enveloping night is prefigured by human beings' doing away with one another in almost vengeful cold blood, without a twinge of conscience, with steady hands, knowing full well that their turn to be killed may come tomorrow—precisely *because* they know that perhaps—it is also foreshadowed by the open market in and the widespread use of all sorts of implements that tear, gouge, and mangle, of instruments that cut, pound, bruise, knock down, bloody, break, and rip apart.

Not all who use these implements are nightworkers. That has become clear.

Somewhere outside town (in what is reputed to be one of the most beautiful places around), at a clearing in a green wooded grove, a place resembling an ancient amphitheater . . .

That is how it was described. Yet I've seen the place and it's nothing like an amphitheater. It looks more like an ancient hippodrome, an arena where bloody games were played, or to put it more accurately, a place I just feel like describing in those terms.

I saw a group of men on either side of an oval field surrounded by great green trees, deep green vegetation, and green rocks, whose clothing, hats, boots, and furs seemed tinted green in the green light filtering through the branches. They lifted their guns in ceremonial attitudes, set their sights, aimed at those across from them, and fired. At a morning hour, when the sun shone with all its might and the sky above the green grove was deep blue and clear.

When one of the men was shot and fell to the ground, tremendous applause rose from both sides and the whole place reverberated. It is said that the shooting goes on and on until only one person is left standing.

19

This was hard to comprehend. It was as if they were taking part in a ceremony of some sort. They seemed to be preparing for a game of chess or soccer. Speaking in low voices among themselves as if they were about to do something important, they took their places at either end of the oval field and, once there, greeted one another nonchalantly across the field, as if picking out their marks, each man confident he was the best at this game.

My chest was tight. I'd run uphill all the way, since passing the last vacant lots at the edge of town; I could hardly breathe. I hid behind a thick tree trunk. I could see the field from above.

I was now among the few who had seen this place that everyone talked about so much.

It did not take the men long to find their positions. They all stood absolutely still. The word *day* was spoken in unison at one end. It was answered by a unanimous *night* from the other. The words added to my confusion.

The guns were raised one by one.

The tree trunk in front of me was dark brown. My clothes were gray. The leaves rustled. The air between the earth and the sky was as limpid as glass. The guns were silent and smokeless. Slowly, one at a time, men fell. On both sides. The body count was kept with huge lighted numbers on a scoreboard atop a tiny building.

I ran away from that place, not waiting for the last man to fall.

20

Nightworkers is a term that's been on everyone's lips for some time. But the opposite term, *dayworkers,* is not in circulation. At least I can say I've never heard it used.

And yet some people have obviously joined together in the name of "day" and strike against those united under "night"— or else children shouting, "Daymaker," make a game of chasing people out of their neighborhoods.

One cannot claim that those killing one another in that clearing outside town, in that richly green field, are simply exercising, or training their hands and eyes. If the event occurs daily, ten or fifteen people must die each day. One imagines that in all likelihood the players prepare and practice elsewhere. No matter how absurd it is to call them players, it's hard to think of a more suitable name. Since the sole survivor of the day must take part in the next day's game, sooner or later he too will be shot. The most he can enjoy is being the hero at the victory bash on the night of his survival.

Yet what is even more difficult to understand about this business is the secrecy under which the players operate. Should anyone be seen near the field who doesn't join in the game or who isn't supposed to join, he's shot at once—so they say. Those who like myself observe without getting caught—this then is also possible, and come to think of it, it seems odd that it's possible—recount what they've seen only to friends they trust. As to whether any of them are punished later, maybe shot, I have no knowledge.

21

When I arrived at the corner of my friend's street, I didn't have to turn and walk to his door. There he stood three paces in front of me. After giving me a blank stare, he glanced at his watch, pursing his lips and looking left and right as if waiting for someone who was late.

I had arrived at the corner out of breath. As I came closer to his place, I had been gathering speed, practically running, driven not only by fear that the children might chase me again but also by the embarrassment of not having looked him up sooner. If only our eyes hadn't met as I glanced up, if only I'd seen him first . . . What would have happened? I admit I'd be curious to know.

The step I took toward him, the words on my parted lips, my arm outstretched to touch him were frozen under his blank gaze. I don't know how I kept myself under control, but I did. I took a couple of steps up and down the street, affecting the confusion of someone who is lost, came back to the corner, and observing my friend's eyebrow twitch as if to point up the street, slowly began walking in that direction. I focused all my attention on catching what he had to say as he went by, assuming it was my friend who was walking briskly behind me. Before I got to the end of the street, he overtook me, turned the corner, and dropped out of sight. What he gave me was a phone number; that's what it must have been. I'd wait at least an hour and then try calling. I thought it would take him an hour to get to the phone, if that was where he was hurrying, and it would take me at least that long to find a place to make the call.

22

FOOTNOTE 3. I'm pressing on heedlessly. The main thing is to keep the reader from sensing that some of these paths won't take incidents or anybody anywhere or, conversely, that only a couple of them will be traveled all the way through. I must take special care. I must make the characters exist and, at the same time, keep them vague. That's the idea, but what does it really mean? For the subject to become vague from time to time . . .

23

Some people find it strange; others don't see anything surprising at all. At first nightworkers were only the subject of rumors and gossip; then a few began to be seen and noticed. But for most people their presence became palpable much later, only very recently, when they came forth to terrorize everybody, hitting, breaking, killing. Yet even at the beginning everyone had felt fear stirring in his gut, everyone (like a patient waiting for the inescapable end of a terminal disease who wakes in the morning to take account of himself and says, Perhaps today will be the same, and I won't be in too much pain; maybe I'll even get through the day . . .—like the patient who cannot give up the hope of seeing daybreak once more as he falls asleep at night), in anguish at the prospect of disappearing at an uncertain moment of an uncertain future, had become accustomed to seeing himself, his friends and relatives, even the pets in his house, as stricken with an incurable affliction. One goes to the doctor even when the disease is incurable. Searching for remedies, one keeps struggling; one behaves as if hope—or a feeling like hope—can never be, has never been, lost, knowing full well all the time . . .

Some people think it odd; others are not surprised at all. People have to have lost all hope in their fellow man to yield to so much fear and anxiety, even when they are seemingly hopeful, trying to do something against all odds. Those who think it is strange warn everybody, adding the reminder that nightworkers are as ordinary as everyone else. But how could anyone who kills so casually, as if it were a game, or anybody who seems to be doing that, ever be considered ordinary?

24

Assaults and murders are often explained, or interpreted, as the result of anger, fear, or repression. Anger, fear, and repression can easily turn into one another, imitate one another, the incentive seeming to be an impulse, and the impulse an incentive. All three are manifestations of an ego beset by feelings of inferiority. Were all nightworkers selected from among those who have been dispirited by continuous defeat? Are all nightworkers people who could not escape their childhood monsters? Are they incapable of embracing their lovers to their hearts' content, or uniting their flesh with the flesh they desire?

There are people who say that or who argue in a similar vein. There are others who analyze the nature of the wave of night that is fast approaching; these find it strange that in the face of the oncoming wave anyone should be prepared to surrender to death.

But there are those who don't find it surprising at all. These people too say it is wrong to give in to fear, since recognizing something as evil is not compatible with acting as if you yielded to fate. But is a loss of trust in mankind behind these people's lack of surprise? If so, their lot is sadder than that of others who at least retain their trust in human nature. Or, on the contrary, perhaps they know perfectly well how capable mankind is of both dread and resistance but are like people who aren't surprised that it rains in the desert though they also know how limited and how fugitive the effects of the rain will be.

My friend was one of these people. Having memorized the phone number he gave me—at that moment I couldn't imagine it was anything but a phone number, and for that reason I call it so even now—I made my way toward the vacant lots (what vacant lots? I should say the countryside), I made my way toward the countryside.

25

The street quit the city suddenly, opening to the country and the meadowlands, as streets can do only in a few Mediterranean towns. This was the sort of countryside where a dusty wind blows constantly, where there are bare, puny, and yellowed shrubs, and dingy grass, and where pebble-sized gravel makes it hard to walk. I looked around but could not see my friend, who had been slightly ahead of me. There were no gardens or doorways he might have ducked into. Behind me, I could see a few scattered houses, but only their windows faced the countryside.

I stopped at the point where my friend had vanished. And after reasoning out the only route he could have taken, I turned and began walking in the opposite direction. I planned to turn again farther ahead and walk through the neighborhood streets once more. First I passed by some houses where most of the curtains were drawn. The path didn't veer off, but soon the houses were far below. I couldn't understand why such a fast-growing city had stopped right there, at that spot, at the same city limit as ten or fifteen years ago. I could make out a path, a vague track, that would take me back into the neighborhoods. But just then a more considerable walkway, which looked better traveled, came into sight; it did not cross through the neighborhoods but instead went up a small hill. I was curious. I had an urge to follow it. I started walking.

At the registry office, they had questioned me on whether I ever left town. Obviously they expected me to. Today what they had suspected came to pass. Sevinç hadn't shown up yet. Had I kept out of cinemas and theaters to wait, I'd have made myself ridiculous. I wonder if I should be pleased that the message didn't say, "Don't go to work. Stay at home."

Was I expecting to see new neighborhoods behind the little hill, or what? I don't know. But I found myself in a desolate place. Quite a way down, there was a thick grove. I thought I made out a clearing in the middle. The sound of paper being torn constantly, augmented a thousand times, rose out of that place. At irregular, unequal intervals.

26

One morning, the crowd walking to work divided at a particular spot on the sidewalk of the city's main square, glanced down without slackening their pace, and then reunited a little farther along.

At the spot they skirted, somebody was lying. It wasn't clear if he was dead, wounded, or drunk or if he had simply been cast there after an accident. He was lying facedown. His arms and legs sprawled unnaturally, he looked like a rag doll that a young child had flung down in rage. His limbs seemed to have too many joints and angles. Nobody went near him for a very long time.

At last an elderly woman put down her bag, bent over holding her knees, then, with one hand on the sidewalk, knelt with great difficulty and gently tried to raise the man's head. People who heard his moans slowed on either side of the pair. The elderly woman put the man's head down carefully and, lifting her own head, began scanning the crowd as it passed. A young man stopped and stood at the man's head; together, they tried to turn him over. The man's moans had changed into muffled gasps. A young boy helped in trying to turn the man's legs over carefully.

The man was lying on his back and groaning softly. His arms and legs were broken in several places. His face was a bloody mess. The bloodstains had spread from his face all the way to his legs; over his abdomen the stain had grown into a huge circle extending to his groin. There were thistles, dried blades of grass, and seeds stuck in his hair and on his jacket and socks, but only the elderly woman seemed to notice them. Her hand went out once or twice to pull them off and toss them away. Then, as if embarrassed by the meaninglessness of her action, she reached for her bag, clutching it by the string.

27

Retreating from the green grove by the oval field where the players killed one another, I found myself farther from the city. The air was so fresh and the light so pure, they scarcely seemed real. Finally I came out on an asphalt highway that must be one of the beltways around the city. I didn't know where I was. I couldn't even figure out the direction that would take me back to town.

For a while I walked on the shoulder; then rounding a turn, I came upon a grand structure. As I neared it, I realized this was the National Library—also known as the Palace of Knowledge—the construction of which we had been hearing about for so many years. I had never seen the building before, aside from the photographs in newspapers and magazines. The decision to build it a few miles outside town had sparked a great debate.

I seemed to have forgotten everything. I walked toward the Palace of Knowledge. From the outside, it was impossible to tell if the building had been completed. Parts of it seemed finished, while other parts had not even been plastered. I entered by the door and, not taking any of the more obscure passages, walked toward the great light up ahead. That immense, sun-filled area was probably at the center of the building, and it was as bright, perhaps, as it was outside. My dazzled eyes counted four stories, with tall railings going around the floors and luminous bands of light surrounding the space. After shutting my eyes to rest them awhile, I was able to perceive the staircases going down on either side. I chose one of them. After I descended what must have been a whole flight, the stairs came to an end. It was still very bright. I seemed suspended on the bottom step. The void below me dropped off into the dark.

28

At that very moment, I began wondering if I was dreaming, but even wondering about it struck me as odd. Just where had I fallen asleep? I tried all the tests I knew. I thrust my hand forward rapidly, I pinched myself, I opened and closed my eyes, I made half circles with my arm, left to right, right to left. I didn't appear to be dreaming.

I noticed the last step of another staircase not too far from this last step on which I seemed suspended. I landed there in a single bound. Trying to avoid hitting my head on still another staircase, which was close enough above the one I had come to for me to scrape my back, I was forced to crawl up practically on all fours. It seemed as if the space between the upper staircase and the lower was narrowing. Soon the two staircases had come so close together that if I took another few steps, I'd surely be stuck. That's when I realized that the two stairways crossed each other. With great difficulty, I was able to climb to the one above me at the point where they intersected. From there the space between them widened. On the first landing, I pointed myself in the direction I hoped led to the door. It amazed me that I found the way out. I no longer asked whether I was in a dream, inasmuch as I was not waking up.

My reason could not take in these unfinished and crisscrossing staircases. All these many years different builders must have executed individual plans for the building, each adding his own stairway before abandoning the work.

29

Lately, nightworkers don't seem to spread out into the streets only as darkness grows and night begins to fall; on the contrary, it seems that squads of them are coming out while it is still light, swinging their short, stout ropes of chain in their hands, and darkness is then falling before it should. We say it must be a sensory aberration, wishing to believe what we say: the days must be getting shorter . . . Are we to think that the sun is adjusting itself to them? Absurd.

The morning crowd that flows through the largest square in the city has gradually learned to discriminate between those who have been beaten during the night, shot dead, and left in the middle of the road and those who simply lie bloodstained, arms and legs usually broken.

Those with broken bones show the effects of an ordeal entirely different from the one undergone by those who have been ambushed and shot: it is rumored that the victims who come out clinging to life were earlier picked from the crowd at random, taken to one of the towers that surround the square, and used in research conducted along what might perfectly well be called scientific lines. People say that what is being measured is human resistance. A newly formed cadre of expert nightworkers who have refined, varied, and augmented the conventional ways of forcing people to tell what they know but don't want to reveal are now investigating how, when, and under what conditions people can be forced to tell what they do not know— things that go through only the minds of the inquisitors—and what accordingly they are in no position to be willing or unwilling to tell. As is the case with all research, there were initially many disappointments, but the experts are sure that as they improve their methods they will achieve success.

30

FOOTNOTE. How can I keep under control the delicate distinction between the character, who is depicted as knowing the inside story but being unwilling to divulge it, and the author, who not only knows and will not tell but also keeps disclosing that he is withholding information? Besides, since I questioned my own strategy some way back, isn't my failure to have resolved the problem itself significant? Corrector, Creator, Author, all remain in the beginning of the book. At this rate, I do not think I'll be bringing him up again. Yet, initially, I had considered him to be one of my avatars.

31

People whose friends suddenly disappear learn to look for them in the morning on the great square; if they cannot find them within three or four days, they wait for them to turn up or be sighted by others at some other place. Unpromising as their hopes are, sometimes incredible things happen. How can there be any hope otherwise?

I wonder about the eyes of the experts, the ones who specialize in extracting information that people don't have. Their eyes must have the frightening emptiness of nightbirds' eyes in the daytime, as well as the sharp stare of predatory birds.

(Strange to talk about nightbirds' eyes as seen in the daytime. Who gets to see their eyes in the dark, aside from their prey?)

Those who get to see extractors' eyes are in no condition to give an account, not as they lie on the sidewalk in the great square.

These eyes, which we imagine as both empty and sharp—what sort of gaze do they have for the mashed, broken, torn, ripped-off, bloody mass of flesh and bone that has let go and succumbed? One has to wonder.

What do these eyes see when they look down at it?

32

FOOTNOTE. While trying to annul time, must we not also dissolve the structure of our speech?

33

After the first years of construction, the excitement over the National Library, or the Palace of Knowledge, has cooled; earlier the object of derision, it is now all but forgotten. Occasionally there is a bit about the building in the media, stating what funds have been allocated for it—as if the construction was never interrupted. Sometimes there is even news about schoolchildren being taken on a field trip to the site—being provided with memories they can recount later. Forget about anybody's trying to confirm the veracity of the stories; it's hard to imagine that there's anyone out there who pauses even to ask whether the building still stands on its foundations. The Palace carries no attribute apart from being a rumor, even though it is the symbol of different things to different people.

How many people, I wonder, have seen as much as I just have?

Instead of turning back toward the city, I kept going south. More than the hour I had wanted before placing the call must have gone by. Had I looked at my watch at the time? I didn't know. It was past four. The road kept improving gradually, soon taking me toward another asphalt highway that was relatively well maintained, although for it to be where it was defied logic. The slopes on either side of the road ahead looked like cuts made with an enormous knife. The wide asphalt highway, at right angles to the road I was walking on, stretched from left to right. The city was probably to the left.

34

Down the road to the right stood a huge building I had never seen or, to my knowledge, even heard mentioned. Parked in front were cars of many colors and models, but all fashionable, giving the impression that the place must be a hotel, a sports club, or a gambling casino. It was as if every one of the city's trendiest late-model cars, which normally were seen so rarely that they drew attention, had convened there, and although each was of a different color, it seemed that every one of them had attracted other cars of the same model to the area. This was a building that went far beyond conventional architecture. Glitter, ostentation, and pomp had been obsessively displayed, with the show of wealth becoming almost palpable. The building and grounds were so elaborate, what with the courtyard, the woods behind, and the gardens, that next to them the palaces of antiquity would have looked austere.

The place was packed with people. All manner of tea, coffee, and other drinks were being served, while cakes, pastries, and other colorfully garnished food came on plates that sparkled with gold leaf. The noise was almost impenetrable. Even so, there seemed to be no difficulty in hearing conversations, for nobody appeared to be shouting. The voice of a famous singer carried one of her most popular songs above the din. Some people were seated at the tables, others milling around or chatting without sitting down. Judging from the stares I received in the parking lot, I was probably giving away that I didn't belong there. My clothes in themselves were dusty enough to attract attention. Perhaps I astonished them by arriving on foot, begrimed head to toe, at a place people came to in cars. Inside, however, there was not room enough to stare at anyone. With great difficulty I made my way toward a telephone I could see in a soundproof booth of clear turquoise plastic on a raised platform. Considering the crowd, I was surprised that there was not a line of people waiting to make calls; then I realized that there were phones in soundproof bubbles at each table.

Everything in this place was out of proportion.

I was having a time of it getting through the mass of people. The floor was raised in places and depressed in others; I had to walk up two or three steps only to step down two or three. When I arrived at the telephone, I was wiping the sweat from my brow. I stepped into the booth and dialed the number I had memorized. The line was busy. As I sat waiting on the platform, my eyes met the gaze of a man seated at a crowded table nearby. I suppose we were both too proud to look away. I redialed the number, but the line was still busy. By the time I sat down again, the man was standing next to me. He was smiling.

He handed me one of the two cups he was holding: "I thought you might like some coffee." I thanked him and, taking a sip, dialed the number once more. Again a busy signal. "No problem," he said. "We'll wait." As I gazed at him, I began to feel self-conscious about staring. "If you wish, we can call from my place," he said.

"All right," I said, "but maybe I should try once more."

The receiver was lifted at the first ring. "Wrong number, sir— for the fourth time!" said a woman's voice, a voice I didn't recognize. "I told you before, it's the wrong number! Please don't try again for a few minutes. Something must be out of order."

She hung up. I hadn't managed to open my mouth. When I told the man by my side what had happened, he laughed. "Won't take us ten minutes to get to my place," he said.

We began to make our way to the door. As we went by his table, he discreetly waved his friends good-bye. "Home," he said softly. His companions must have read his lips. We got into one of the best-looking cars. As the engine roared to life, he said, "I'm Sevinç. And you?"

35

FOOTNOTE. This notebook is done. What is it that I hold in my hands? At most, one view of the world. So?

II

36

In one sense, everybody is an enemy. My enemy. Our enemy. Or will become our enemy one day. Our friends, for example, our confederates. We must mortar the foundations of our lives with doubt and suspicion; we must make these our daily bread and water. Even so, we have to believe there are four or five people in this world who will not disappoint us. A few people to constitute a touchstone on which we try each doubt and suspicion, a grindstone on which we sharpen every strength and action, a keystone by which we keep hope alive. When they tell us to shoot, we'll shoot; when they say die, we'll die; when they say live, so we shall. They will be a stay not only for us but for the whole world. We must believe and put our faith in this.

Our opponents keep telling us that our leaders are human, that they too can err and do ugly things. But our opponents don't understand that a mission may choose its man. Persons such as our opponents have forgotten, or have never felt, never learned, respect, belief, and trust. To have to call them persons brings home the sad inadequacy of language. They aren't even persons! At most, they are God's mistakes, his rough drafts.

Even if those who command us aren't free of faults, blemishes, and errors, we must emulate what we find in them.

37

We must emulate the faults, the mistakes, and the blemishes of those whose commands make us who we are—not that we are to think in these terms (we must not), but let's assume the hypothesis of their blemishes for the sake of proving to our opponents that we are not in lockstep to the degree we are accused of. What those we follow do, after all, is what it's necessary to do if we are to reach our goal. Whatever they do, we must do, or at least try to do. They have no time for anything but our objective. Even if they had, they would spurn the trivial. An attitude of superiority is the sign of magnanimity: man evinces a superior attitude to the degree he is magnanimous. But doesn't the most infallible measure of greatness concern setting the precise limits of that attitude? Doesn't greatness lie in knowing better than others how to draw the delicate line between the thinkable and the unthinkable?

Men have forgotten greatness and the gulf between it and mankind. Many others have said it before I—before we—have: we live in a world of bewildered dwarfs. It is all that nonsense about equality and such that has brought us to this pass. How can there be equality if it is contingent on doubt and suspicion? The only possible equality to be established one day will be equality in duty, in obedience, and in the dreams of our greatness. In our love for Him who commands us.

My father had many faults and inconsistencies. But I will never forget his respect for the mighty. Does anyone know the meaning of such respect these days?

38

If truth be told, I can imagine having to change my thinking, but I cannot hope that my opponents will ever get closer to my thoughts.

I think that either the past is a frozen state consisting of a set of unchanging elements when you take a cross-section of it (at most, it can be freshly interpreted; in order to explain it, we may examine it from other points of view), or it is a pure confection of selected elements of what has been—especially those elements we favor or disfavor—put together side by side. It is not impossible or illegitimate to take this construct as reality and to apply our current thoughts toward actualizing it. But no, we just cannot get that through their heads. More correctly, they don't want to grasp it. They insist on promoting their own constructs . . . not that theirs have any clarity. Theirs are a hodgepodge, utterly eclectic. Some of the elements of the constructs have yet to be seen, or to put it more accurately, I don't know of any history where they are recorded. I certainly am not going to harp on what is recorded in history and what is not—especially not here. But the evidence our opponents offer is so persuasive! Here is the point, and the only point, where our thoughts are superior to theirs—and it is a clear superiority: we can prove that each element of what we assert, even if it is a construct, has been realized in the past by taking the appropriate steps.

But then, regarding events about which history makes definite pronouncements, are we not especially prone to a number of wild dreams that start, What if this (or that) were (or were not) the case?

39

From now on I will call him N. No longer is it of any consequence whether his name is Naal, Nait, or Nahi. His name and
mine mattered when we were kids playing in the same schoolyard, sitting at the same desks, and having been ever so careful
to keep quiet, getting to read the same adventure book during
study hour without being scolded or put in line. Our names,
his name, were the chief means of distinguishing us from the
throng around us. Today I can call him N. I know that he is of
no account, but even though he does not think as we do, he's
not one of those who would string us up either; what's more, I
know he's not someone who'd be interested in getting hold of
the noose. I am also quite aware that his arguments against us,
spoken in his dispassionate and level manner, can be more dangerous than anyone else's exhortations. I know that the words
he speaks with hesitation in his hoarse voice can be convincing;
I have listened to him enough to know. He doesn't incite, he
convinces. Even if his words are soon forgotten, the residue of
his discourse stays in his listeners' minds.

I have a feeling he is content to think of me as He: I am
somebody, and he knows it. He must be at least as unhappy as
I am that we have been reduced to single sounds, phonemes, on
each other's lips; I'm as sure that he feels unhappy as I am of my
own name. He does not have the means to keep track of me,
but I imagine he at least reads my work. As for me, not only do
I read him, I also watch him in the most unlikely places. Those
assigned to watch him, without awareness of one another, are
directly under my command; I am the one who transmits their
information and reports upstairs, that is, to the extent an au-
thority exists above me.

40

He is not aware, of course, that I saw him at the Palace of Knowledge today, wandering through the cavernous spaces wearing the bewildered, almost tearful look of a child who has lost his way.

He would have no way of knowing that my office is in the string of secret "core rooms" where the light is supplied from above by reflectors, through a technology significant enough to gain mention in the annals of architecture, which I've named "light stacks." In this building, which has stood incomplete for so many years that its existence is almost forgotten, the core rooms are hidden in the space between the rows of outer and inner offices, all of which have windows.

I saw him approach on the TV monitor. We wreak all kinds of havoc on those who arrive unexpectedly. The kinetic staircases, which were designed against fire, are perfect for our purpose. Most likely he will never know that he got out alive because I knew and recognized him. If he found out that he had arrived at the planning center of the Sun Movement, at its very brain, what would his face look like? Imagining his expression makes me want to laugh.

It was obvious he had not intended to come here. I am quite aware he does not embark on extended excursions that would bring him all this way. According to the report, he was last seen on the street where his friend used to live. He would have no way of guessing the person he saw there today was someone wearing a plastic mask to simulate his friend's face. He could not possibly know that his friend was one of our agents who, no longer willing to cooperate with us, had been sent to the rifle range several weeks ago. I also know where he went after leaving here. Most probably, he passed by the rifle range. I do not imagine that his will had any part in our success in getting him to take that route.

41

During the war years, privation afflicted both our homes equally, as I easily inferred from what he once told me. Was he less conscious of it than I? Or did poverty just sting me more? I could not say what his parents talked about at home, what they taught him.

Our conversation at a class reunion years later helped me correct what I'd thought as a child and explain to myself what I hadn't understood.

Every text, and every life, has dead periods, dead areas, and dead points. But N seemed to live in a continuous state of nullification. His thoughts, his writings, his behavior were not harmful in themselves, but it was the quality underneath them, what I have termed nullification, along with the reticence, bashfulness, and secretiveness it carried, that was more dangerous than anything else. He was in disaccord with everything, with life itself; alongside his outsider's apprehensiveness, disconnectedness, and humility—I think I can say this without falling into contradiction—he had an audacity that bordered on shamelessness. I understood later that his so-called submission to fate was something other than humility. Even though he lived in poverty and experienced impoverishment for years and still does, he is resigned to everything because he has no expectations and no desires. But he can still be excited by abstract thought, even if only once in a blue moon . . .

Our activities make him furious sometimes—that is what the reports say. But he never attempts to do anything about what bothers him, nor does he sit down with anybody to thrash out what we are doing with any thoroughness. Ever since I've been shadowing intellectuals, none of my spies have dug up any real dirt on him.

42

As if shadowing intellectuals weren't enough, I attempted to become the deeper self they'd hate to see in their dreams, let alone in the mirror. It is wrong to say deeper self; I correct myself. I should say their deeper I's. The deeper part is all right, but aren't we in the business of getting rid of the I?

A man who accepts defeat, subjection, and oppression is not a man in my book. He is subhuman. Had I not relied upon the directness, the power, and the allure of my conviction, and had I not drawn the leaders of the Sun Movement into believing in it, I wouldn't be where I am today.

They called me a sore loser when I was a kid. Let them call me names, I told myself, I may get beaten up, done in, but I never accept that I've been defeated. I always find the power to wrest strength from the stronger. N would just as soon be defeated as win. Or even sooner. He was not interested in games as a kid. "Let's play backgammon," I challenged him once when we were older. "But beware, I'll beat you."

I will never forget his response. "Since it's a game, you either win or lose," he said. "No problem."

I was appalled. I went through with the game just for old times' sake. But I don't consider him subhuman anymore, because he reminds me of my father. Besides, I know that what he does is not accept defeat but, rather, refuse to let it bother him, or when you come right down to it, not really play the game. But games are a serious business. I want him forced to give the game everything in him; I want to see him do what my father didn't. But if he still won't care, I'll let him be. Not only that, I'll provide him with wealth beyond his dreams, I promise, given that we're bound to be in power for another couple of generations. But if he should buckle under . . .

43

FOOTNOTE. Is it the author who cannot make up his mind, or the character? Is there only one character speaking in the first person in this notebook, or at least two? To what degree can I make use of the indefinite number of speakers or, to resort to a conventional expression, the inconsequence of the character? I *must* confuse the reader; he must be confused and scared. More and more I have a feeling I could hold the whole world in my hand. A feeling that I could keep the I's of the most disparate characters in my palm . . .

44

If he accepts defeat, I will hold him responsible for destroying in my heart the father who destroyed himself in my eyes. Then I will kill myself. But before I do, I will come down harder on him than I do on all the other meek put together. Until the very end, as he gives up the ghost, even if not much of him remains to toss into the grave, I will administer the different (I didn't say it right: not the different but the variety of) tricks I, and my experts, know and dream up . . . without ever showing myself. Just before he dies, when I see his eyes (like all those who know they can no longer survive the pain they have adjusted to) relinquish this world (and I trust he will be no different from anybody else), I'll make my presence known. Will those empty eyes then come to life for a moment?

I will reveal myself to him alone. It won't be important, since I'll die soon after. To him alone, for there's no pleasure in secrecy that is never bared.

It is a matter of public knowledge that I direct the Capital City Research Center. But no one knows that the center functions as two separate organizations. My underlings have no idea that the greatly revered Capital City Research Center knows nothing about them.

As for those on the green field who prepare for death with the abandon that the mastery and the mysticism of marksmanship require, they have no knowledge that most of them, almost all, have already been condemned to death. Each of them knows only that he must obey orders and slay a particular person across from him.

45

The constant destruction of the teams that appeared to kill one another—and this illusion had to be kept intact—was what shook the equanimity of the board of directors, because of the cost and, of course, the slaughter of all those peerless master marksmen. It was certainly difficult getting such a project approved. But before we started working on the larger project of the research center, I wanted to see whether our leader would defend a proposal of mine that, anyway, demanded less secrecy, and I had to find out whether he would live up to his commitment not to divulge under any pressure that the project originated with me. I was the kid who sat next to the best student in the class, and even copied from him in a pinch—indeed, was not above misleading him—not because I did not study and had a poor grasp of the material but because I had to best the very best. I could not let anybody outshine me. Now that the same kid has become the movement's brains, he has to do it right, even manipulating the leader when that's called for.

Getting the game, the ritual, of marksmanship accepted was difficult. No one could see its necessity. It was a long and arduous campaign to persuade the board that a secret movement re-creating the general dread that had secured the success of the old mystical orders could also help the ostensibly overt Sun Movement. In a sense, it was the power that rumor could have that brought them around at last. What imbeciles! The whole lot of them.

46

FOOTNOTE. Housing a second organization within the research center without any word of it leaking out is difficult enough.

It might be plausible to keep what is called the Sun Movement more or less "overt."

The Palace of Knowledge is designated an official building. Using it for covert activities makes the difficulty even greater.

But then, at this point, does anything like that matter? I put "credibility" aside a long way back; a concern with it might subdue a writer.

47

Give people something a little mystical and a trifle poetic; provoke the feelings, sensitivities, and sentimentality they have long forgotten or buried away; stir up the childhood fears, griefs, and timidity they think they've outgrown. And have them do whatever you will. Then it is easy to obscure inconsistencies that are clearly visible and to deny the multiform subterfuges and intrigues kept hidden. If anyone notices and tries to speak up, call it slander, defamation, and mudslinging. Backbiters like them deserve whatever treatment they receive! Even death! Never mind that all these poor fellows have done is penetrate into or figure out something they should not have. That is all.

The job of the brain is to project circumstances in the way they appear through our eyes as well as to eliminate those around us who are not ready to identify with our vision—or else, before rubbing them out, to use them to dissuade others who persist in seeing things with their own eyes. The eyes of sight, of course, have nothing to do with the vision defended by the Sun Movement's steering team. But that must not be known either.

Secrecy, or covert involvement, is one of the oldest and most primitive bonds that can hold people together. Given the nature dominion takes in the contemporary world, we know that imposed force is not enough. People's hearts and minds must also be conquered. We also know that secrecy does the trick—secrets within secrets, in levels, in frames, in boxes. Something has to be concealed, provided that there's someone who knows the secret. At this point, I am that someone. What if there were an attempt to keep something from me? Am I sure I'd find out? I simply cannot imagine not getting wind of it.

48

"It never occurred to me he might go inside. But he did. The place was off limits to us, so I crouched down between the cars and waited. He didn't come out. I had another guy take over the watch. Must be that he has friends in there. Looks like he'll spend the night."

I have no use for anybody who writes this kind of drivel. Had it involved someone more important, he would have found himself on the rifle range. In view of his gifts, keeping tabs on N is just about the right job for him. I couldn't possibly entrust him with the surveillance of someone more dangerous.

"Must be that he has friends in there," indeed! How absurd! The stupid spook couldn't be expected to know, of course, that N has never associated with the people in there, the oldest of whom is at least twenty years younger than he. He was probably in and out in a flash, flummoxing our dunderhead, who'd better go back and post himself in front of N's house.

He did not call the number we had given him. The one that sounded like a telephone number. Odd. Or maybe not. Had he put any thought into it, he would have figured out the number's significance . . . the meaning it has for just the two of us. Inasmuch as he didn't call, has he caught on that the number has nothing to do with the telephone? If so, he must realize what the number is. But then, what can I make of his failure to act?

The kids who frequent that place are as unaffiliated with us as their families are affiliated. The families believe that their money controls the world and consider us curs who are fed on meaty bones, unaware that their turn to become curs will also come. For the kids, though, we have become so familiar that they are not even aware of us, like stage sets that can be easily knocked aside when they decide to expand the scene. We have to wait a while longer before acquainting them with their error. The Sun Movement is not their dads; it is us.

Odd, isn't it, how people are apt to trust their fathers, families, kin, and friends, assuming that only *small* skirmishes are to be waged against them.

49

"The five roaches became one hundred, one thousand, then ten thousand strong. At first they were nesting behind and on top of cupboards, under the shelf paper, in the corners of drawers, and around pipe fittings; then they invaded newspapers, old paper, and books. Next, they began practically jumping out of bread boxes, cooking pots, refrigerators, and people's pockets. The sight of cockroaches sallying forth from under pillows and sheets, as if they had waited for this to happen, made the bug-killer manufacturers rich overnight. No roach spray remained at the grocers, markets, wholesalers, or factory warehouses. The bugs, which spread out in armies, scurrying out of every door, box, house, and store in the city, dived into dishes of food, into water, laid their eggs in every available spot, and hustled around oblivious to the people flailing helplessly against them, undaunted by the countless victims they left behind as the clouds of insecticide reached the streets, making people cough, cry, and gasp, as well as robbing them of their sexual power. But even if the populace had had all the bug spray in the world, the situation was already out of hand. People could be poisoned by these compounds, but the roaches had become so numerous that they were ineradicable. There were probably still a few people somewhere who did not take the trouble to spray the bugs, but even if they were to come to their senses, they would no longer have any recourse."

He didn't think the article merited his own name and published it under a pseudonym, yet it is perfectly clear who wrote it.

50

For some reason people show pretty peculiar ideas about their own worth. They pretend to be modest but then take umbrage at the slightest remark or decide that something they've produced doesn't measure up to their self-image. They get angry at those who criticize them, and they put pseudonyms on their articles. People who don't have the honesty to be pleased with themselves, and the soundness to show that they do, are the lowest of the low. I have to say that this goes for N too. I say it but . . . At the time the cockroach story was published, no one would have been offended by his article or taken him to task. He used a pseudonym not because he is timid but because he does not want to put his own name on a story he does not think worthy of his signature. In a sense, his is a kind of hypocrisy. Telling a tale about what's going to happen to people through the allegory of proliferating bugs or animals is an old trick. He's sophisticated, our gentleman, and sniffs at such devices, judging them stale. Should we take offense at the story in the first place? I've been brooding about that for quite some time. And every time I ask the question, I arrive at the same conclusion: yes, we should. That quiet strength of his that I have called nullification, his acceptance of whatever may come—which must be based on the idea that everything, starting with himself, can perfectly well be imagined not to exist—makes him more dangerous than those who stand up to us openly, kicking and screaming. Am I giving the man too much credit? His immunity from anger, or the temporary nature of his angers, which are like flashes in the pan, is unsettling . . . A person has to be capable of rage and aggression. A person has to have ready a set of unshakable, unchanging examples in order to get his dander up. How is someone able to live if he doesn't find examples when he looks back and doesn't create them either?

51

"Examples are fictions we create with this or that motive in mind—sometimes with yet another lurking behind it—out of the inexhaustible ocean we call the past. After convincing ourselves of the reality of such a fiction, we try to convince others . . ."

Which one of us wrote that? Neither. Yet either one of us could have, following it up differently, of course. I had the man who wrote this definition given a beating three days ago. Right in front of his house, too. He must know by now that we take the business of conforming to examples, as we call it, very seriously. I don't think he will ever write anything like that again, or if he does, no newspaper or magazine will publish it, at the risk of getting torched.

Our methods, I must admit, do have a drawback. We create false heroes and champions, in symmetry with our own heroes and champions, as if in a mirror, but completely reversed. Instead of examples, we create reverse images looking at us. Which mirror will reflect us for ourselves? We seem to be on a perpetual march past the distorting mirrors in a fun house.

After we've created an example and convinced ourselves and others of its reality, how can they accuse us of molding our lives according to criteria that we have not forged ourselves? We do not try to emulate our fathers and our past; ours is the only way people can be forced to do many things that must be done. But they pretend not to see it. Why? The work people we revere have done in the past, more than inciting to emulation, gives us heart. How timorous is action without examples!

52

This notebook, in which I make a one-page entry in my minute hand each night, has become something of a headache. Suppose someone chanced upon it. I'd like to see him read it! Let us imagine I dropped it at home, in the car, here, or left it behind on a table. I have no qualms, given that everyone knows what fate may befall him who reads it. My name is on the cover. Besides, whoever finds and returns it should know that I'll be informed and that he may be sent to the rifle range. Even so, I cannot shake the feeling that someone might try reading it on the sly. Am I dead sure no one is watching me? A person having me watched might be someone I will not ferret out until the day I die. A man can only take measures against what he can imagine. But what about what he cannot imagine? I am quite aware that I may have, indeed, that I have, limitations. The thing is to try to expand your boundaries constantly. A man is most vulnerable at home. I spend every other night here, feigning that I have work to do, and stay right on top of my buttons, my computer, and my countless hands and feet. Naturally, I have my own examples, which I have created for myself.

For three days now, N has covered his tracks. Interesting. Could it be that he's given me the slip? Maybe he's out getting his rocks off. In whose bed, though? How could I not be informed? Sevim claims that since the day she took him to the Ministry of Trials, she cannot find the minutes of the question-and-answer game she had him put through. She is one smart girl. She devised the game herself and won me over. Could it be that something has gone wrong at the ministry? Sevim is the only agent I can run as if she were two persons, each at war with the other. She will succeed with this business, too, no matter how difficult it may be. Must start with the ministry, first thing in the morning. Must move heaven and earth to have N located.

53

For quite a long time now we've been acting as if we agree that the only topic of debate between us concerns the "making of falsehood into a system." Or should I say we had been so acting? Whatever happened between us many years ago has been left behind in our childhood. We're mature people now. Yet, looking at his behavior and life-style, one concludes that either he has not grown up or he is, in a sense, challenging me. He has no qualms about openly maintaining relationships that others would want to be clandestine or at least find embarrassing. He says what's on his mind without trying to discriminate between what may be said and what shouldn't be. He will not even seek protection by marching under the banner of freedom of thought. What is more, I'd stake my life that he no more enjoys getting blamed, disgraced, or criticized than I do. I might even say that he is trying to buffalo me by parading his associations in the open. But, for some reason, I do not believe he is trying to hurt me—at least not as long as he doesn't see the necessity of causing me harm (that is, until he decides the time has definitely come to overturn my system of secrecy, smashing it and killing me). The more I attempt to create a world in which each thing hides something else, trying to convince everyone that the world should be so, the more he argues that people and actions must wear only their true faces. Yet people are more afraid of what is covert, or unavowed. People must feel the grip of fear.

54

People should stay within a severely limited code of morality; they must believe in the virtue of renouncing what they desire. It is only by being under such pressure that they can identify their enemies, or the worms boring within, and put up a real fight.

Purification is necessary. It is the movement's foremost goal. Besides, not until a purge takes place can other work be advanced. Purification must convince everybody that no matter how thorough and massive the cleaning job, the evil, the corrupt, the enemies among us cannot be easily flushed from our midst but will lie in wait to catch us inattentive or indifferent. That is why we must be constantly vigilant of their slightest movements.

Those who spend time at the Club R should not be fooled by its location out of town and its familiarity only to those who frequent it. They consider themselves such privileged creatures that N must have thought he'd stepped into an entirely different world. But their time is just about up, too; that they have no idea about it does not change a thing. Perhaps his arrival there will bring the end both for him and for them. I can think of three or four possibilities, but in every scenario both they and the place are in for a fall. The ensuing hubbub will be suppressed as the movement takes its most decisive step yet toward gaining control over everything. We will regulate history not the way they think but according to our intentions, as we've shaped them. But the purge will not be over.

Even if purification hits *us* some day, the cleanup team will have just enough time to gape at the cleanup I have in store for *them*. Just about enough time!

III

55

I know it's wrong, but I can't help thinking from time to time that I wouldn't be here today, in the thick of things, if I hadn't dared make fun of him when I was just a little girl. Were the two of you more than just close friends? I'm still not sure. Back then, I was too naïve to know what might be involved in such a relationship; among friends, we talked our heads off about things we didn't really understand, and this was one of those subjects. He was a man I found attractive, so I said those words that day just to tease him for being so unabashedly conceited. His reaction was rougher than I'd anticipated or could have imagined. Soon after, I became his wife. And although he was my wedded husband, he all but raped me. We were divorced a couple of years later, but in reality it was only our beds that became separate. Otherwise, we still work together. Now that I am his assistant, we see each other every day, sometimes for hours. His wife, the one who came after me, learned to accept the situation and feel no jealousy only after many years. Today, thinking as a woman in my prime, I'm not far off the mark when I say I'm his true wife. What I said years ago that made him so mad concerned you as much as it did him. I don't know if you ever knew. But you never came into my life, or became aware of me; you had already drawn away long before I arrived on the scene—that is, if you were ever truly part of it. Yet your shadow—I must call it that since I cannot come up with another word—has never been absent from our lives.

56

This time my assignment is considerably more difficult. For quite some time now, I've been trying not to let either my work or my emotions weigh on me. Since I became aware that anyone, nearby or far, can feel or suffer many times over the hurt, the trouble, and the joy I experience, I've been attempting to blunt in my mind and in my heart even my greatest pain. It has been seventeen or eighteen years since I've thought this through, which coincides, almost, with the time I was divorced. All this chatter is empty in a way; at most, it serves to let you know a little something about me, and that is the reason for allowing myself to write. Yes, as I was saying, this assignment is considerably more difficult. I am sure anyone would think so. What's more, succeed or fail—that is, if I decide to do it according to instructions—it will be, can only be, my last job. I must die or escape or become someone else. I would have to become someone so entirely different that fleeing would be easier, but then death seems the easiest of all. Even if I should be forced to kill myself . . .

If I have managed to learn to write at all, I have learned it by reading the two of you. That is the truth, yet obviously I'm not a student worthy of either. Even so, I persist in writing. But, after all, this isn't really writing. So don't be too hard on me. Getting these papers through to you is easy for me. The trouble is I can't quite figure out when reading them will be most useful to you. In a few days, whatever form my fate should take, I will no longer be myself. But until that day comes, I'll continue writing to you. As to getting them delivered . . . I'll think that over.

57

My intention to disclose to you a matter that's top secret, as secret as anything we can imagine for the moment, will put me in jeopardy. For whom is it a secret, and according to whose point of view, I would not, in truth, be able to tell you. To all appearances, I am a civil servant. My boss also appears to be a civil servant. But the work he does and the work he has me do are completely outside official channels. "Secret." Yes, according to *our* point of view. But then, who are *we* really? Even so, here's what I say: If the establishment of a system conceived by one person is conditional on keeping secret a project imagined and implemented by two, requiring the silence of both, then we are in the presence of some people who view themselves in a magnifying mirror. We have inflated ideas about ourselves. How right people are to be angry! How right you were to write the piece about the cockroaches, neither admitting your authorship nor hiding it. Yes, we convinced ourselves that we're a big deal, but we still have to toil night and day to assume the slightest power. We are doing our best. I am troubled, however, by how dirty the work is becoming.

For a long time, our plans have kept coming up against three obstacles: A great number of people are against us. A fair number scorn us. Even those who use us, or think we are useful, almost outnumber us. We put up with being used only because we believe we will ultimately take control. I still believe that strongly. In our estimation, we are right; we want something sublime, and we aim to get it. Yet the dirtiness is an objective fact. We manage to dredge up what we have to in order to put the killing and maiming of people in a favorable light. But we cannot be proud of planning and perpetrating on a national scale the meanness that was once the mark of small-time palace intriguers, can we?

58

Many have already said that great work cannot be accomplished on the basis of small-visioned moral conventions. Pounding it home that ethical codes have to be made even more stringent, have to be tailored to the cases, and contending that the necessary process of purification has to be exempted from restrictions, we've arrived at the point of wanting to adopt, even among ourselves, the intransigent attitude of someone striving for absolute dominion. Using mystery, fear, intimidation, and terror against others, we've suddenly had it dawn on us that we're using them with fullest force among ourselves. Today none of us is ready to go back or give up what we've won. Yet some among us at least know that it is always possible to come back from beyond what are thought to be the points of no return, provided that we try not to look ahead from where we are standing but to look at where we are standing from up ahead. It's tough to do but not impossible. Yes, at least a few of us still know it; we have not forgotten. But it seems as if we will soon forget.

What I am trying to explain is so involved that I'm not sure I can. Let's imagine a board game. The black pieces must win. On the same side as the black, there are red and yellow pieces. Facing these are the green, the purple, and the white. Exchanging pieces at the rate of one for one would take too long, and might not even ensure victory. How play the game so that each black piece can capture not only two or three white pieces but simultaneously take several red and yellow allies?

I confess that, with his help, I came up with one of the most ingenious solutions to this quandary. But, you see, I can hardly be proud of myself.

59

But I did make a contribution I am proud of. Something you also mentioned in one of your pieces, although I don't think you were aware of our plans. That's the reason I bring it up.

You know when the kids in your piece called "Night Knitters" assigned roles for a game, saying, "You be the crook, You be the cop, You be the spy," and told the darkest one among them, almost a black, "And you be the night." I found the idea truly childlike, but what you went on to say was so contrived it was unworthy of you: "Those among the adults whose patient hands knitted the night on long needles first knitted stitch by stitch the wool of fear; the skeins of fire that would burn them, too, waited in their bags for their turn." Reading that, I felt my suspicions aroused. Were you trying to tell us that you knew something was up? I came to the conclusion, though, that you had no more than an inkling about it.

Yet fear was the emotion we truly intended to use in, if you will, a scientific way. As you very well know, we employed it in various forms, but as I said before, I am proud of the form it took in my "contribution." Our principal objective was to push the young people who had committed themselves wholeheartedly to the movement into a contradiction. On the one hand, we made sure they felt that even their most extreme behavior would not jeopardize their position, that nothing could really be done to them, and on the other hand . . .

60

I know you didn't recognize me the morning I took you to the Ministry of Trials. Certainly, you couldn't be expected to recall a friendship with a schoolmate of some thirty years ago. I'm aware that what I'm saying is presumptuous. But since you're one of the people we follow especially closely, I've tried to learn something about you. I've drawn my conclusions from what I've heard and what I've learned from reports. You consider the past and whatever has happened as things you'll keep—or discard—the memory of only after passing them through very peculiar filters. I'm not putting this very well, but since you were not affected in the slightest by a remembrance of me, let alone a recognition, I know I've got it right. The degree to which words and faces interest you, or somehow bother you emotionally, determines your ability to remember them. You live as if in a dream, forgetting your own words as easily as you forget those of others.

I didn't expect you to recognize me. That's why I could volunteer to come and get you. Besides, as you'll understand, this job could be done only by me. But I was somewhat apprehensive. It was possible I was retained among the things you didn't forget, your memory hinging on some small detail that I did not recall myself. At the very least, you might have given me a brief glance, meaning, I know her from somewhere, and gone on from there. But that didn't happen. To tell you the truth, I was a bit puzzled, and in a way sorry, that you had no idea of my role in the dissolution of your friendship with him. I realized, however, that we would never cross your mind, even though you'd be playing the leading role in the game we had planned for you.

61

On the other hand, as I said before regarding the young people committed to the movement, we made sure that they felt besieged by enemies. It may seem absurd, but to those who know the inner workings of fear, it is not absurd at all. It causes people to run wild if they think that their excesses will go unchecked. Feeling beset, they end up making more enemies, but they can't help feeling righteous for defending themselves against a sea of foes that keeps swelling in their imagination. While you are engaged in the most ordinary and innocent of activities—say, something like writing for or publishing and distributing a perfectly legal periodical—if you come up against a wall of enmity, even if it is your own creation, you'll resort to whatever guile or force you need. Fear and vengeance will surge inside you. Not bad, after all, I think you'll agree.

I am aware that I keep putting off what I mean to tell you. I keep dragging my feet. After all these years of training to toughen feelings—or lose them—I don't know why I'm in my present state. As if it weren't enough that I am writing all this to you . . .

In three days, you will be sent abroad. We have been unable to notify you sooner because we don't know where you are at present. We already know what you will say when you hear this. "Not like this, unprepared . . ." But we will still persuade you. There isn't a soul that cannot be persuaded. Especially you. You have been known to say, "The hell with it," and go along with things you don't like, simply because you're sick and tired of being harassed. We know that too!

62

FOOTNOTE. People expect others to respond to pain and suffering the same way they do—or more accurately, people won't even entertain the notion that reactions other than their own are possible. That is why pains cannot be shared even insofar as they are more than purely subjective. We manifest and defend our jealousies, dissimilarities, and irreducibility most ardently on this point, and it is also the point at which we are most contemptuous of others. Would our behavior and attitude change if an instrument could gauge that we suffer exactly the same pain? I doubt it. We would simply prefer not to believe the instrument.

FOOTNOTE TO THE FOOTNOTE. The footnotes have once more changed character. Nevertheless . . .

63

For hundreds of years, although we have never forgotten the power of the nail, the fist, the bone, the muscle (or of their extensions), and have used it every chance we've had, exalting it obliquely or even from time to time openly extolling it, we have also denounced it with incredible hypocrisy as a power we must rise above, repress, and eradicate. We teach that reason and understanding are the only path to take, the highest plane to attain. What is happening now is nothing less than the revolt of our nails, fists, bones, and muscles against this dishonesty. Now we are avenging them; we are forthright enough to do it and throw the hypocrites' deceit in their face. The power of nail, bone, iron, and terror will once more be respected. Where that force is rendered sovereign, everything soon falls into place. Everyone recognizes his limitations, his capabilities. People learn to submit to consolidated power.

Yet, all this is so contrary to your views, isn't it?

Anyway, I'd better cut this short. Today I'll seal the envelope in which I keep all these papers and get it ready to be sent to you. Sending it to you will be one of the three last things I do before taking off. Today we finally established your whereabouts. When you are given your instructions, you will be asked to leave without delay. The official who brings you your traveling papers, and your instructions on how to behave at the conference you are to attend, will be one of my men. He will also give you this envelope. After the officials leave (an assistant official will also be present), I hope you will read these papers instead of wasting time talking to your companion. I have no idea whether you'll feel surprised or not, but I hope you won't let on too much to your companion at once.

Here is what I wanted to tell you all along:

It is well known that you are against us. But your being one of the three to represent the country at the conference will have far-reaching consequences both here and abroad. If you should refuse to go, five of your friends—who are guilty of nothing except emotional involvement with you—will be picked up on an official pretext and altogether unofficially pressed into "giving you away." The whole affair will later involve legal action and will be leaked to the press, although in a very different form. Thus we'll see to it that you're subjected to the official process. It will be too bad not only for your friends but also for their families and all those who "follow the same path." If you do go, you'll be too proud to "skip out" before the conference is over, I am sure. You'll persevere for the sake of the voice of intellectuals like yourself, if not for ours.

I may be wrong, of course. But if you should think of walking away from the conference, just remember that we won't be standing by with our hands in our pockets.

On the evening when the conference is over, you may feel a temptation not to return with the other representatives and instead to remain abroad a while longer. The other two will retire to their rooms to get ready for the trip home, leaving you on your own. It would not be surprising if you harbored the fancy that you are free to do as you please.

We know you are very fond of taking walks after dark. You will probably venture out to places, cafés and shops that you are familiar with in that foreign capital. But soon after you go out, you'll be shot by the agent assigned to tail you. Not fatally, just enough to wound you very seriously—at least that's what we expect from our gunman, who is one sharpshooter. While you're in the hospital, it will be disseminated that the gunman was an enemy of ours who was incensed by your participation in a conference attended by one of our declared supporters and by another delegate who at every opportunity states that he is not against us. I've already arranged a swap for our gunman. But as you know, exchanges of that nature are made on the quiet. You are free to do whatever you like once you're released from the hospital. We sincerely hope you don't die.

Ultimately, we'll reap an enormous benefit from the public outcry resulting from such a heinous murder attempt by our "enemy." Objectives we could otherwise have achieved only through repression will suddenly fall into our laps. You can easily guess what is involved. The interesting aspect of this operation is that we will be furthering our own agenda under the guise of official business, and no one will be the wiser.

Naturally, all this may change the moment you read what I have written you. I believe it will. It doesn't seem likely that my agent will open the envelope. But it would still be a good idea to factor in that possibility. Anyway, whether he opens it or not, what I am doing has already placed me beyond the pale. Don't bother about why I've told you all this. Perhaps I've already communicated my reasons, although at this point I cannot gauge how successful I've been. If the official reads this, you won't get a clue about anything. Perhaps I'll be able to hear news of what happened to you where I intend to hole up. Who knows what dirty tricks are still in store for you and the others? I wish you'd go ahead and open the envelope immediately, rather than be fooled by the instruction stipulating that it be opened on ". . . / . . . / . . . at . . . o'clock." What more could I ask for? There are limits.

IV

64

Coincidences are always strange. Especially if you're sure they are genuine coincidences. Writers like you "depend on facts, practically discounting all irrational activity"—a tendency acquired partially from their education, as with most, if not all, intellectuals. Yet they are inexplicably attracted to the irrational and that which lacks a factual basis. They openly display the attraction they feel, as if challenging the world. They feel a pleasure akin to what people, in their delusion that they're free, feel as they move unresistingly toward what has been forbidden them. In this, writers are even more gullible than children and are taken in by incidents that would fool no one else. As in, for example, the coincidence of our meeting.

The odd but true thing is that I like you very much. I have always held you in high esteem. When I read your work, I felt respect because you said openly what I had never ventured to others; you also spoke in my behalf, defending my right to live, although you didn't know me. I would never have dreamed that one day I'd come up to you and say, "Let's go to my place." I was already prepared to like you. Even if you had been someone I'd never heard of, I would still have taken to you right away and suggested that I take you home. What is odd is that the task was assigned to me.

You began addressing me familiarly after the first ten minutes. I know you are not in the habit of using the familiar form of address. The note in your dossier regarding that had attracted my attention. Even in this utmost intimacy, I will continue to address you in the second-person plural—even though my generation is in the habit of addressing everyone familiarly and is willing to use the formal *you* only in a very rigid relationship of subordination. In a way, both of us have gone beyond our established habits to give the other special treatment.

Too bad that it wasn't coincidence that brought us together. Even though I am young, I consider myself mature to the extent that I don't make irrational statements. Then I go and say something irrational.

I've always dreamed of meeting you, and here I am, closer to you than I could ever have imagined possible. Yet I end up regretting that the meeting was prearranged and not coincidental.

Isn't that incredible?

65

FOOTNOTE. Now that I'm divided into four, to what extent can I count on achieving the symbolic reach my grasp aims at? Or rather . . . But no. Being unable to know what to say is senseless.

66

But that's not all that's incredible. Recently I was almost given the assignment of trapping you into saying things you don't think at all. I'd decided to come back and tell you everything and then shoot myself—perhaps you first and then me. Or I'd made myself believe that was what I would do. They eventually gave up on the idea. My present assignment is merely to give you these messages. According to the instructions on the one envelope, you are to open it in seven days' time, but the large envelope is to be opened immediately and the contents read. I beg you, open and read them both right now.

After the long phone conversation of mine you overheard this morning, I said to you, "I'm going to the grocery store." It wasn't true, of course. I went two doors down the street to pick up these envelopes.

67

It was before nights and days got tangled together. I had been ordered to meet you and hand over two letters. You were walking on a deserted road. If I'd hurried, I could have overtaken you. Back then, my days and nights hadn't yet tangled together. I didn't want to be the sort of messenger that sidled up to you in the countryside. I risked everything and drove my car to the Club R, taking the back road from the Palace of Knowledge. It was possible that you'd never turn up. But I could always find you later. I was the one who called out the phone number as I went by and then dropped out of sight. At that point, I had to masquerade as your friend. Somewhat embarrassed, I had taken off the mask in the car. When I called in from the club, I was ordered to burn the letters at once. I burned them, in plain sight of everyone, telling them they were love letters. The lie eased my discomposure. I was through with the assignment when you arrived. You went up to the telephone booth. I still don't understand why you got that answer. I came to you. My days and nights had not yet become yours.

68

You didn't say what the envelopes contained. Since you didn't hide your reactions as you read, I knew they brought you some very astonishing information. I don't want to ask, I don't want to know. Please, don't get me wrong. Now that I've delivered them, my duty as a messenger is again over. If there's anything I can do, any problem that I can forestall, tell me, I beg you. I don't know about you, but I could be shot as I walk out the door. Who knows? The days we spent here together were perhaps part of someone's plans and calculations. I just don't know anymore. When nights and days tangle together, and you become one with another, the unbelievable and the believable dissolve into each other.

"At least, it does not yet seem as if we will be shot, Sevinç. It seems that we will be together a while longer."

69

FOOTNOTE. Things are getting out of hand. Good. Or bad, perhaps. But whom do I take myself to be? Have I made up my
mind?

70

The way I express my emotions, or rather, the range of emotions I express, or, who knows, maybe both, appear to surprise you. Yet when we first met, you didn't seem surprised at all. Tired like a child who repeats his lessons to himself, I'd tucked my assignment away in a far corner of my mind; I was trying to contain my excitement. You seemed almost to be expecting me. Until you heard the name Sevinç, you couldn't possibly connect my presence and anything you might have been told previously.

There was a gleam in your eye when you looked at me. I must thank you.

You see, I'm sorry I owe our coming together to someone else's machinations, and I keep trying to make myself believe that you were waiting for me, that you were searching for me although you didn't know me. I'm aware that you may cringe at my lack of restraint. I imagine that you will find fault with me, but since you don't behave as I wouldn't expect you to, I try to provoke you. I talk nonsense in the attempt to convince myself that I can swim in these dark waters where I struggle to stay afloat.

I know we cannot remain here much longer. We will have to leave. You will have to leave. Even if it takes you hours and days to come to a decision, you still must . . . we still must . . . leave. Days and nights will again untangle themselves, they will follow each other within well-defined boundaries. As night descends, hollows darken first; and they are the last to receive the light. Yet I love light, I used to love light. Once. Now I want night to embrace me. I must become hollow, stay in the hollow. Maybe someone is digging my grave now. But being thrown down into it means not ever to see light again. That's what I regret. I'll keep quiet from now on. I'll do what you say, go along with whatever you decide. What saddens me is that I may never, not ever, see you again . . . I will not open my mouth again.

"I leave tonight, Sevinç. We leave. You'll see me off. But I think we'll meet again. I hesitate to say I'm sure we'll meet again."

71

There are those who do not flinch, who give no shudder, in the face of the suffering and pain, the murders and massacres, the death and carnage that they read of in the newspapers, or hear about in conversations, though they're aware that they ought to feel anguish. These at least worry about their lack of feeling. But there are others who not only never feel a thing but don't realize that anything should be felt at all. These not only don't worry; they don't understand why anyone should. They are not heartless; it is just that their imagination is incapable of going beyond their own trouble and suffering, beyond what they can touch and see. That is all. The same people get emotional, become upset, and weep when they come across the picture of a crying child or watch a mawkish movie or play or read a maudlin story. Their imagination can be stirred and awakened only by a certain variety of tangible experience.

There are people who, after a pretty good time in bed with someone new, cannot bring themselves to answer the question, When can we get together again? They look away, or look for excuses . . . They like their partners; they might even think they could get along with them—if they make the effort to think. But at the decisive moment they cannot get beyond a twinge of discomfort and a whiff of shame. Their real trouble and failing is again perhaps their impoverished imagination and stunted fantasy. They are like brutes who cannot imagine ever being hungry again once they've torn into their food and swallowed it whole. They are altogether unable to taste anything properly, or to give it its due. You'd think they didn't rise to the level of conscious awareness, for they seem not to know what they really want or to foresee what might happen in a few hours or a few days.

It is an ignorance of life. An ignorance that makes one say, "It's no skin off my back," or when confronted with the pain of somebody one has no feelings for, "He had it coming! Serves him right!" It's a poverty of thought: The poverty of those who can read but don't know that they're not alive, of those who cannot imagine that a person can concurrently participate in many different modes of existence. A poverty that can sometimes be mitigated slightly by being down-and-out on the street, or face-to-face with baseness.

72

FOOTNOTE (!) (S). Your attitude seems one of trying to silence me or, rather, of trying to cast me out of your book. Yet, when the actual model for a character puts in an appearance, there is little that writers can do. Easy, isn't it? Making anybody do or say whatever you want! I have nothing against the freedom fiction writers enjoy, not I. But doesn't it ever occur to a writer who bases a character on a real-life person that the original will object to being used like this? I know. You'll say that whereas what you write will survive, the real-life model will perish, lacking, even if eminent, the "reality" of the fictionalized character. But is that really true?

Anyway. I cannot tell whether you'll finish this book or not. In your present situation, neither can you. Perhaps you couldn't get it done even if you wanted to. But then, perhaps you will. No one has come to a decision as to what will happen. It might take a day, or six months, but there will be a decision. But it certainly won't be to release you. That's all I can say.

In a way, these notebooks could trigger a decision, even tonight . . . if they are seen and read, that is, if some eyes manage to see and read them. At least, so it seems to me. But no one will see these notebooks, I promise. Don't laugh. This promise is nothing like the promises you put in your writing. But you too must promise you will show these notebooks to no one. You have to protect yourself.

Every day, as long as we stay here, you will show me what you've written. We will talk and argue. Let's say that I am curious how you will bring it all together. Let's say that I enjoy seeing you give people I know different guises. It will be to your advantage to show me this notebook, without anyone else's knowledge, when you've filled it up. Besides, I've already read the other notebooks. When you're done with it, leave what you've written with me; I won't destroy anything unless it's utterly unavoidable. Who knows . . . at least your name may be cleared some day. I'm dying to see what you'll do when you wake up and see my words in your notebook!

73

FOOTNOTE. For some time now I've been feeling endlessly reflected in a hall of mirrors. I no longer know what happened to whom, or where the door—the exit—is located. My footnotes have lost their meaning. Some other hand has dipped into the text. That which had been my book appears to be riddled with so many holes that anyone can sneak into it anywhere. We'll soon find out where this will lead. Who in the world is this character who fills up notebooks? I'm puzzled—or act as if I am. What for? I don't even know that, it seems.

74

Where does night begin, and at what moment? Who among us has been able to decide? We speak about it through metaphors: night's impending arrival, its descent, its embrace, its yawn. We have all understood by now that night is closing in and that we will be crushed. Yet who among us has ever owned up that we're just shamefully deceiving ourselves a while longer, entertaining the childish hope, however vain, that awful things will not happen, that we can evade the inevitable even as it confronts us? I bet none of us ever has. The fact that I keep writing as if it were still early in the evening, even when I know full well that night has already fallen, can be explained by the special liberty of fiction. It is easy to say that the storyteller has the option of taking up the story at whatever point he desires. But do I not surrender myself to false hopes and consolations even as I choose the beginning of the story?

Night slowly spread over the plain (as I wrote before), then it swallowed even the hills. When I mentioned the underground palaces, I was thinking of the gyms that some of the big buildings are reputed to have in their basements, designated for physical training and various contact sports. When I wrote all that, in a fairy-tale atmosphere, wasn't I striving to affirm my right, and that of my readers, to remain skeptical? (Whoever my readers may be . . . Do I really conduct myself as if anyone would read me? Or . . .)

I wished at least to believe I would have some readers. The only thing I can be certain about, however, is that apart from myself there is only one person who will, or can, read my work. And that person may well not destroy my notebooks. It is up to me to make a decision. Should I tear up and burn these notebooks at once and eat the ashes? Or should I finish the work, let him read the notebooks, then destroy them? Or should I just leave them with him?

75

Write for the sake of writing. Write in order to keep in practice. Write even though you are undecided what to say. It is imperative to write. This book must get done.

If some people are seized and, for punishment, have their bodies hurled through the windows of shops whose owners have also been marked for punishment, and if the sight of moaning men lying motionless among shards of glass like bloodstained dolls broken beyond repair produces no effect other than to make those who pass by shudder, and if undesirables are thrown into the street from windows ten flights up, then I have to finish this book.

Without worrying about who will read it. Instead, worrying about how to go on with the book that has been started. To find a way of continuing the story without tearing out the last few pages and still having it all come together. To write, for example, the following: "I will try imagining the four of us in bed together. I will try to visualize the four of us in bed, making love, without manhandling one another, without tearing one another apart, having transformed all our lingering grudges, anger, and thwarted selfishness into love. It is only then that it will be fully manifest just how ludicrous our behavior is. Since we constantly lie to ourselves and to those closest to us, since we are, in fact, obliged to lie to ourselves before lying to others, since we have set up a world where everything turns into sham situations and false feelings, it is necessary to carry these lies all the way, pushing them to a point where they explode. So that we become unable to lie anymore. Or we die."

76

Maybe it was childish to think that by opening the second envelope and reading the contents, I'd arrive at a decision in a way similar to that in which a person decides against going out because of an inauspicious omen in the cards. But maybe it wasn't. I could be up against an intricate plot designed to goad me into doing something I would almost certainly have decided against. If it was a trick, I have fallen for it.

But anyone who plays games of this sort must be fairly confident of winning. Yet those messages did not spur me. I was curious if there was a way out. Who knows? I kept hoping that in planning everything so thoroughly, pretending to be gods of some sort, they somewhere slipped up. I wanted to continue to think it was possible for them to be humiliated, or at least to look ridiculous.

Perhaps I don't look exactly ridiculous, but I am in a trap. What is worse, I may have walked into the trap willingly, that is, like a fool. Is there anything else I have to do to look foolish in their eyes?

The hope I felt in landing at the airport of that foreign capital turned into a feeling of being contaminated as I observed the expressions of confusion on the faces of those who met me, and understood a little later that beneath the confusion lay suspicion. I felt an urge to bathe immediately. There was a second bed in my room at the hotel; I wondered playfully whom they would put in that bed, knowing at least that it would not be Sevinç.

When I came out after my bath, Sevinç was lying on the other bed.

77

Has it ever occurred to you that the man next to you (in front of you, across from you) will require a grave proportional to his stature (height, weight, girth)? that he will feed the creatures underground to a degree proportional to his size? that his body's growth since birth is proportional to the love, care, effort his progenitors have put into it? that the fight and struggle of the person to keep his body fed (although "to keep his soul fed" may be a better way of saying it) is proportional to the supposition that life is a matter of eating and drinking? and that, in reality, all this is nothing more than an elaborate preparation for death?

While thinking of a corpse that by consuming the share of one or two others has grown more appetizing to the worms, maggots, and bugs that swarm over it, have you ever considered that all that the man who carried the corpse's frame ever did in life was struggle to become such a magnificent, imposing corpse that those who bore it to the grave had to sweat and founder under its weight? I wonder.

But all this goes through my mind every time I see an overfed person. And I am gripped by an anxiety mixed with nausea anytime someone says, "You have put on a little weight." If sensing—especially sensing—the impossibility of building one's life without building one's death is considered a sign of illness, I couldn't care less; we keep preparing for death no matter what we do, after all, so it must not be extreme insanity to envision what balances a life.

I keep thinking neither Sevinç nor I, nor even my antagonists—I am not wholly unaware of them—will turn into the sort of corpse I have just described.

78

I turned off the light on the little table and stood in front of the window. There wasn't much light outside.

I waited for Sevinç to come to me. We had not spoken at the hotel since our arrival. Naturally we had to talk at the meetings, when others were present, but when we were alone we could still embrace perhaps—at least one more time—but we couldn't speak. From now on, opening our mouths, even to ask for a glass of water, would be lying.

I waited for him to come. I heard him get out of bed, the sound of his bare feet approaching on the rug. Then I heard the tapping of his fingertips on the table right behind me. Obviously he was hesitating. He always does that when he's at a loss about what to do: he'll drum his fingers on a table, a book, a door, or a chest. The sound was different when there was no cloth; this table had a covering made of velvety stuff, or rather, more like a woven rug, so the tapping was odd. His hand reached for my shoulder. I didn't move away from my position in front of the gauzy curtains. I wanted to see him naked once more, perhaps for the last time, in the dim light coming in from the street. I could tell he was naked from his smell and his warmth.

His hand stroked my neck. I turned toward him. I grasped him by the waist and pulled his body to me. Before I arrived here, I could have thought we were parting once and for all—when, for example, we rose from the table at which we had our tea at the airport, or just before that, when I boarded the airport shuttle bus . . . But we came together again, and then again. I must be fair; it's possible that he did not know this would happen. Perhaps there were new orders waiting for him at every turn, and he was merely complying with them. We were together again, but this would have to be the last time, or almost the last. It could not be any other way. I wished we could go on standing in front of the window. He probably wished that too.

Then the force of my arms caused us to sway backward. His body pushed against mine. My thighs were pressed against the table behind me. I had not expected the two jabs of pain, in my leg and in my back.

79

Sevinç was always with me at the hospital. I cannot recall what he had to say. For quite a while I was not allowed to speak. It turned out that my wound was serious . . . my wounds. They asked if I had seen my assailant and instructed me to reply by blinking my eyes. (I knew who had had me stabbed, perhaps I even knew who did the stabbing, but I had not seen the *hand* that stuck the knife in me.) The door to my room was not locked when they found me; it must be that I was stabbed when I stepped out of the bathroom. My companion had been awakened by my moans. I was told all this on what I guess was the third or fourth day in the hospital. I had been told in the letters it would be a gun; no mention had been made of a knife. Either they had altered the initial plan or I had been given misinformation. Their course was reasonable, since it did, after all, prevent me from speaking on the second day of the conference. If I accepted that as a premise, I had to get it through my head that it had been a game all along. Believing what any one of them told me had been naïve. Sevinç was with me. Was he waiting for me to get well enough that we could return home together? Or, more pointedly, was he there to haul me back? In that case, what was the use of any of this nonsense?

I have often thought that as long as we understand something, there is no way it can defeat us. It has been a mistake to rely so completely on this idea. Now I am beginning to know defeat. Because I no longer understand. I cannot explain what I don't understand by presenting it in a different guise, can I? It has been some time since night has covered the scene. Now I find myself on ground so completely unfamiliar that I'm unable to find my way in the dark even by feeling my way. They still will not permit me to speak or move. Will I ever be released from this place? . . .

80

(Even in retrospect, I must write as if reporting the events as they occur.)

Today they permitted me to sit up. We are talking. They apologize. They tell me the person who stabbed me eight times over has been apprehended and convicted. Sevinç is gone. He left three days ago to return home—as I was told, "back to your capital city." They must have put me to sleep and kept me sleeping. I do not think I passed out. I have no knowledge about anything at all. Nor do I understand anything. An intolerable light floods the place relentlessly.

I am not preoccupied with my wounds. And I am not told much about them. Books, pamphlets, and reports and minutes from the conference are stacked beside my bed. I am told that I may read but that I must not tax myself.

I couldn't care less. I let myself go. After coming out of night to arrive at a place where there is true daylight, it is ironic that I have ended up like this.

Some time later, I am told I may get up. I feel a strange tightness in my chest. One of my legs is dragging.

Then I find myself on the street. I seem to be walking unsurely. There is too much light. Someone takes my arm. "Take a seat," he says guiding me to a café. We are brought some coffee. The man tells me he has been assigned to protect me: "You almost fell down. Actually, they did quite a job on you. We were all very happy that you survived. What are you thinking of doing now?"

I am not thinking of doing anything. Would you like to talk to some people? "Like who?" I say. Besides, who is this man? There is no one I want to talk to. "It is too light," I say. "Let's find ourselves a shady place."

"We are already in the shade," the man says.

I tell him I wish to rest. "Certainly," he says. I am all

too familiar with the hotel room he leads me to. The second bed is not occupied. The man says he'll wait downstairs. I visit the bathroom. When I come out, Sevinç is lying on the other bed. He seems to be sleeping.

81

At times we are sick and tired of running, chasing, loving, making love, living, dying—or watching someone else run, chase, live, and die. We can always find a reason, a credible, persuasive, warranting justification for any action, or for the refusal to act. Or we keep thinking that we can find it. Then, one day, our justifications are shaken to their foundations and collapse. Even dying loses its meaning. A desperate condition by comparison with which falling down a bottomless well whose opening has long since been lost from sight can be considered happiness.

After exhausting yourself in declarations about night's repugnance, you discover one day that light bothers you, that you seek, first, shade and, then, darkness as if it were a sheltering warm bosom, or a lap in which to take refuge. That is the day you find yourself in my desperate condition.

Returning to night (Sevinç!), meaningless things becoming even more meaningless, knowing that you have become a toy—of dubious usefulness—in some people's hands, not knowing in just whose hands . . . either I am going mad or they really are after me. They are after me with a vengeance; they are trying to push me over the edge. In that case, shouldn't I ask why they take so much interest in me? Doesn't the question deserve a satisfactory answer? So long as the answer isn't forthcoming or isn't sought after—or following this line of thought, so long as the answer is evaded and avoided—falling into a bottomless well remains the image of happiness. Or have I been reduced to a state in which I fool myself and, what is more, don't even know it?

82

The writer of fiction is supposed always to know where what he writes is heading; at times even the writer believes this, or is led to believe it. Yet the writer must never forget that he can't be sure of the next sentence until he has written it down.

I keep forgetting that I will not, cannot, leave behind a finished book, one that I recognize as complete and worked out all the way through. I do not think I will be able to leave this place. Not soon. Even if I could, there is someone posted at my door who would keep my notebooks as a souvenir. Even if they let me go, won't they want to use the notebooks for intimidation, as if shaking their fingers at me from a distance?

Leaving these thoughts aside, I must never lose sight of the fact that what I'll be leaving behind is a rough draft. *Only* a draft. That leaves me room to maneuver, doesn't it?

How smart is it to go beyond the bounds of fiction and introduce my own views? But why should such distinctions concern the reader? . . . I should say, the *person who reads it*. (How quickly a writer becomes accustomed to the idea of an "audience"! This time, though, there will be no audience but only a solitary person who reads it, perhaps.) There is no reason why the person who reads this should bother to keep the particular ideas of the writer, when he can make them out, separate from the rest instead of seeing and investigating all the different levels as a whole. Have I not had my fun teasing readers who look for traces of the author in his work?

A draft. The incomplete. Remember, one is always ready to be carried away—rightly or wrongly—by the hope that a better version can be produced in the future.

Only a draft . . . A handy phrase. What distinguishes a finished work from a draft? Apart from what I believe or think it is?

83

For a long time, I kept my schooldays out of my recollection. I wanted to. And I was successful: I put up a masterly resistance against remembering things that others wanted me to remember, refusing to concede that I did recall them. Lately, however, for some reason I have been looking back on those days and the people I knew then. Especially N . . . It is no longer significant whether his name is Nemi, Neri, or Nezi. I remember him as N. That makes his name seem more interesting, since it seems to stand for a number.

He was a kid with short rusty blond hair, freckles, and intensely green eyes. He went to school with us for four years. Even when we changed classrooms, he wouldn't change his seating in relation to ours. We always sat close to the door, in either the first or the second row, but he took a seat in the back, next to a window or in a corner. Each year he chose a single friend for himself, walking and talking with that kid alone. He'd lean against a wall in the schoolyard, watching the rest of the kids run and play but wouldn't get close to them. Only that year's friend was permitted to come anywhere near him; if someone else, someone not familiar with this quirk of his, came near, his face, with its habitual frown, became even longer and closed up totally.

He was deaf. But he read lips with great skill. His attentiveness made him popular with the teachers. He didn't study hard, counting on his infirmity to see him through. That's what riled us. He was allowed to pass all his courses. We resented him but did not let on. We ended up excusing his aloofness on account of his handicap but continued to be offended by the way the teachers were so gullible. It was simple for him to free himself from our company. He could do it in a flash. All that was necessary was to turn his face away and refuse to look at our lips.

84

N and I rarely spoke during our four years in school together. When he missed school, he'd ask us for our notes and the assignments. We sometimes wondered why he asked for them. Were we wrong to think he was a lazy student? We assumed he only wished to dupe the teachers, but maybe he was keeping up with the work. Or since he had no friend except his chosen companion, maybe he was trying to forestall our hostility at least, although indirectly, by flattering those of us who were admittedly good students and took good notes. As far as we could tell, the prejudice of others, which gradually turned into antagonism toward him, did not trouble him greatly. When he wanted something from us, he behaved as if it hadn't crossed his mind that we might turn him down. After the illness he suffered as a baby left him deaf (according to the information we got from the friend he chose his first year), he must have been given everything he asked for. He'd start writing as soon as he felt he wasn't being understood, because certain sounds came out of his mouth slightly distorted. (Still, I was always astonished that he spoke as well as he did.) He always had pen and paper ready. His notes employed either the imperative mood or the indicative.

The year after he left school, he wrote me letter after letter, insisting that I was his friend for the year. His father's job had taken the family to another town, where he was going to school. But he must have found my correspondence unsatisfactory: when we met the summer after we graduated, he greeted me indifferently and then wandered off. I'd never have thought that one day, many years later, he'd distinguish himself as one of the night's principal workers.

85

FOOTNOTE (!) (S). You've really been doing your best to screw things up royally the last few days. You found me, that is, the character for whom I think you used me as a model, in your room once again, and then you dropped me. You interjected a deaf schoolmate into your account without any reason to. Did you just want to imply that he's become a very important person? The name of your game is mudslinging, if you ask me. And then, inexplicably, you assigned the initial N to this guy, a letter someone else appears to have used to designate you. At first you seemed to be dealing with current affairs, creating a general atmosphere; now you're attempting to insinuate yourself into everything, parading out a few characters and endless plots and schemes. You think that you are, or that the person who presumably is you, is everyone's chief concern and main interest. Yet you're aware that your success hasn't been dazzling, given, as you've mentioned, the question that remains to be answered.

What will you do next? What are you thinking of doing? Sure, you can shape the book any way you want; after all, you're free to degrade yourself as much as you choose. No one is going to stop you. But if you think I will give up reading what you write, then think again. I keep watching you, from here. I see whatever you do in your room. If you write, I'll want to see it. So it's best that . . .

Your sort cannot escape the clutches of our sort. Don't let the fact you haven't come to grief in the time you've been here fool you. If we haven't destroyed you yet, it's only because you're not especially remarkable. We just don't have to explain why we bother with you.

86

I must admit I've locked myself in a vicious circle. But not because Sevinç wanted it so. Initially I tried to work out a basic sequence of events. But things overtook me very quickly. What I wrote, or later on, as chapter followed chapter, what I planned to write, was about what could be seen. But what is not visible began to loom more important. What mattered was no longer that night fell over everything but the ways taken by those who prepared the night.

Someday the whole matter will be analyzed, from many different angles and in many different lights. I'm in no condition even to begin an attempt at that kind of study or investigation. At most I'm capable of providing a few bits of data. That's all. Concerning just a couple of things not many have seen or heard about, which only a few would dare mention even among those who have. One cannot really call what I'm putting together documents. Those who study documents would not bother looking over what I can offer. At most, everything that I'm writing will serve only a few people as a single document.

Nightworkers have not stopped at beatings, experiments, and murders. Not even at creating fear, terror, and exhaustion by using this or that kind of pressure. They proceeded cleverly, and with little or no commotion seized one by one all the bastions and strongholds they had to control. They managed to identify people, groups, and entities that, although not affiliated with them, could not oppose their actions in specific areas; they were careful to keep these on their side every time they took a step, employed coercion, or enforced a new ban. The nightworkers knew how to take advantage of their silent collaborators even when by their silence they were the ones to lose opportunities, even when they were the ones directly affected by a ban.

87

If those who project onto various objects the feelings and emotions, angers and murders, hidden so deeply in the recesses of their hearts, flesh, and nerves that probably even they (who interpret their cowering fears, inadequacies, constraints, resentments, and hungers as objects or enemies) are unaware that they are there—if those who project their feeling in that way attempt to equate history with themselves, then surely the end of one world has come. It means that for some doomsday has already happened.

There have been more than a few people, and more than a few eras, just like that.

Those who founder are submerged by falsehood and injustice. (Who knows? Maybe someday someone will denounce these lies and wrongs.)

It was soon after we returned. Newspapers and magazines were publishing long accounts of what had happened to me. It pleased me greatly, though, that not a single picture of me appeared anywhere. But I found it interesting that they had waited for my return before reporting all this. While news about a small incident of two months before was being palmed off as timely, it was being used to implement other schemes that had long been in the works. At least, that was abundantly obvious to those who make it their business to interpret the news.

Seven days after the initial onslaught, the news on the subject came suddenly to a halt. There was no more talk about it or about the "persons involved in the incident." Then, one morning, at my door . . .

That was the morning I was picked up at home. Later I was brought here, to this place that looks more like a hospital, a mental hospital, than like anything else. I am not allowed to see anyone. I do not have any idea what is going on outside. I just have a feeling that people are savaging one another.

Why was the corpse of the woman deposited in front of my

door? She was the woman whose name I once thought might be Sevinç, only later to learn that she was called Sevim. They must have taken pains to have the body look as if it had been dragged out of the building. That was the account I received. On the morning the body was found, however, as I watched the rush of passersby from my window, I was thinking that . . .

88

Until just yesterday, even as I started these notebooks (I can say, "until just yesterday," since I am talking about such a recent past), I used to believe that every action that we perform, everything that we write, and every day that we pass through, had to be carried out, composed, and lived as if we were building a wall or weaving a fabric of the finest quality and the most skillful execution, taking care to make it so flawlessly and so tightly that each stone, each stitch fit perfectly with the others. I used to say the greatest achievement of mankind's struggles in a mortal world was to build, to weave, to do one's share, and then to leave it to those who followed. That, I thought, was defying death and acting as if it didn't exist.

I am in no condition to know if I am wrong, but I suspect the fabric has been torn and the stitches have come undone, the wall has begun to crack. Under my touch the stones and the threads are coming loose. Sticking these stones back in place and tying the threads back together—does it seem *beyond me?* No. But it definitely seems *futile.* Something not worth doing, not worth bothering with . . . As I get to the end of this notebook, it comes to seem idle to offer explanations, to make connections, to worry about continuity and well-formed sentences. We must, perhaps, give up thinking that writing is a tool (or medium) for bringing order to a disordered world (that is, exterior to any other order imposed by the human mind) or for engendering the fallacious notion that it can do so. Writing and speaking and doing will not reconcile us to the absence of order, an absence that we can no more than find strange.

89

Has there ever been an era that was not confused (or complex)? I want to say, I don't think so. But I just don't know. During even the most disorganized, the most hopeless, and the darkest periods, people have emerged to transmit the notions and deeds considered most worthy of being handed down, even if the way they conveyed what they wanted to was incomplete, stunted, disjointed, skewed, even wrong. For some reason we cannot properly grasp the significance of this kind of transmission—as in the effort to teach a child or an adult at least to read and write. We are well along on the path of considering schools and books, writing and words, ever less meaningful than the most recent (here and now) successes of technology. We are apt to forget that facility with the written word is part of the transmission. We assume we can pass along a matchless set of words in flaw-less works and well-crafted texts, thereby reasserting mankind's victory over death. But in a life squeezed between two infinite oceans of darkness, it's our mistakes and misapprehensions that provide us for a time—don't they?—with our false sense of se-curity, at least until we become aware of the two darknesses and ponder them. I suspect that the person whose hobby is to untie tangled knots usually fails to see the insignificance and the de-ceptiveness of the comfort his hobby provides him. The thought does not even cross his mind. The point of view—why not call it what it is?—the lunacy that thinks it possible to bring order to the chaos of the world, and the complexity of the human being, makes some among us, maybe all, imagine victory. It consoles us. We are confident that what we write next time will prolong the victory as well as enlarge it. When will we give up deceiving ourselves and others in this way?

Having written this, have I given up the attempt myself?

Sevinç will be the one to give some answers.

90

The night awakened the fears that slumbered in people's hearts; it kept them awake. Both the people and their fears. We can be sure of that.

That man is a creature of only daylight is a myth. Who among us can deny having savored the anticipatory pleasure of morning, whether when unable to get a wink of sleep or when, having repressed all fears, sound asleep in the hope of reaching daylight once again? Yet the night is a return to the cave: it is swimming in warm waters, the return to a time preceding most of the deceptions. Even if night itself is contingent on a lie.

I don't know what the woman called Sevim attempted, but they didn't waste time in adding her to the roster of those who have been murdered. I don't know how or when they killed her. I heard nothing. I was writing my daily lines in this notebook, and for that reason I was deaf to the world. What most people find so difficult is so easy for me! . . . That must be when they killed her. Who says she has to have cried out? They may have sneaked up on her and caught her unawares. Even somebody else might not have heard anything. If they used a gun, they probably put on a silencer. But why was she left on my doorstep? As if she had been killed inside and then dragged out?

What did they gain by killing her? Who knows how many more are slated to die? Would Sevinç tell me that, as well?

91

Can creating a work of art, achieving something great, be considered more significant than knowing how to live a good, rich, and well-rounded life, and succeeding at it?

What I have written is not flawless; I have not produced anything that can be thought extraordinary. On the other hand, I have not been able to make a good and well-rounded life for myself, either. Everything is half-baked, my work, my life; that is all I've managed.

I see that the nightworkers have been completely successful. At first we thought their plan to drown us in an all-inclusive darkness was childish and crazy. Every idea bears the dimensions of the mold, or the terminology, in which it has been cast. Such a desire as theirs, which seemed radical and extreme to everyone but them, was articulated in their terminology and contoured to their mold. Repression was their chief aim. Figuring out that they would succeed even if they employed the most ordinary means was perhaps their greatest accomplishment.

92

The days were over when a person—or two or three or five or eight persons—might be killed, when among the bombed and strafed crowds many perished and many more were wounded, and when human blood had lost its fundamental retaliatory value. No one was being killed anymore. Or else they were but no one heard about it. The gait of those who walked in the city streets was perhaps slightly swifter; instead of walking aimlessly, people seemed to have a specific destination in mind, perhaps somewhere at a distance, which they wanted to reach by a certain time. Their movements were possibly a little more rigid; they seemed strung tighter from head to toe. Not looking left or right, they pivoted their whole bodies when they needed to look, turning their chests and bellies along with their faces—as if their backbones were not articulated. No longer did people look at one another. It was as if eye contact had been forgotten. No one looked away, it was just that no one appeared to see anyone else. Everybody gazed vacantly, eyes staring at a point beyond, as if whoever was encountered was transparent. Could these vacant-eyed people with their vacant expressions have a reason for going somewhere? (I describe them as vacant eyed, but if they had looked at one another, would they have observed that there were no eyes in the sockets, these people who, if so, could be considered blind by definition? I can almost visualize such a situation: creatures who *look* at one another to *see* that they are eyeless.) Since no one heard of failures in the basic municipal services, some among the walkers must have gone somewhere to do their jobs.

I was content to observe all this. Content with my observations. I had no business at any government office. Why should I? Besides, others may have observed in me what I have seen in them: taking a look at me, other people may have thought my gaze or my eyes, too, were vacant.

Since I took a lot of walks during that period, there was at least one person wandering the streets who did not feel anxiety about arriving on time at a particular destination. Accordingly, shouldn't that be how he appeared? But it's absurd to speculate about what others may have thought when they looked at me.

While people walked rigid and vacant eyed, the streets were regularly being dug up (on the pretext of making repairs and placing or replacing pipes) or raised or lowered, their access to other streets cut off. A tangle of dead ends had begun to spread from the center toward the edges of the city.

The city started to thin out, acquiring a new aspect.

93

Theoretically we accept that our eyes, our minds, and our thought patterns may be inherently arranged so as to lead us to incorrect conclusions, but for some reason, on top of being unable to see our mistakes, we judge ourselves very shrewd for not taking the word of those who point them out to us. We resist recognizing that even what we consider basic truths may be neither basic nor true for someone who is right there before us if he is inherently unlike us. We arrive at our theoretical concession of this possibility only by becoming aware of the disagreements that conflicting thought patterns can give rise to.

The rich do not show off their assets, they use them. (The newly rich may initially be tempted to put on a display, but they soon learn better.) We who have no direct experience of wealth assume that the wealthy like to flaunt it.

The beautiful carry their beauty with their heads held high, untroubled to be ogled for their beauty, but those of us who aren't beautiful are upset by the natural and immodest exhibition and are likely to complain that someone beautiful is unspeakably vain.

Our wish is to see no one distinguish himself or cause any upset. We forget that this sort of fear of disorder lies in ambush only in barren hearts.

In my world, all kinds of beauty and all kinds of wealth must come together, each being only a colorful piece that with the others can form a pattern. So that I can believe I hold the entire world in my hand, that it will not slip through my fingers. If it slips through, everything will be over. If each line I write sounds as if it came from other mouths, other pens, I will become the whole world. I will be all.

I found some papers in the envelope where I keep my notebooks. I am copying them in random order. When were these things written? And by whom? Did I write them?

94

In addition to the tangle of dead ends, something else was spreading over the city: the rumor that, with all the streets being repaired or about to be, the city would end up a maze.

One may think it absurd that rumor could attach to work being done in the open. But it is well known that the city's inhabitants are all too willing not only to spread rumors that create anxiety but also to believe them. It's true that they pass the rumors along not as if conveying news but as if murmuring to themselves about an impending danger that might lead almost anywhere. Yet it's legitimate to call it rumor when what you can see being done in this or that street is magnified into a mysterious plan being imposed on the whole city, especially when those who describe it that way have witnessed virtually nothing.

The streets were ripped open and excavated, and the pipes underneath were dug up and replaced or repaired. But after that activity, which everyone could see, something also struck even the most casually observant when the municipal workers—or the workers who were thought to be, who had to be, municipal workers—pulled out as if the work had been completed: the paving at one end of each street was still at its original level, but at the other end it was invariably at least a couple of yards above or below the street that crossed it—or that used to cross it. That is, it was no longer possible to enter a street and expect to leave at the other end; instead, it was necessary to go out the way you came in. The main streets seemed to be suspended in air. Certainly it was still possible to turn into at least one side street off each main avenue, or so anyway the townspeople thought, but more often than not you had to walk the entire length of the avenue to find out just which street could be taken. No one even thought of driving a car anymore. Eventually people became accustomed to not leaving their houses unless it was absolutely necessary. Those in on the city's new geography could easily zero in on anyone. All they had to do was, perhaps, wait a little.

I was walking briskly that evening, trying to get to the Avenue of Gaps. But I turned around quickly when I reached the end of the street I was on, because I saw that the avenue was some four yards below the sidewalk where I stood. I skipped the next street and took the one after it. The darkness there should have told me something. This time the street ended up three yards below the avenue. I had to be home before dark. For several days a rumor had been circulating that those who were out on the streets after dark were lost for sure.

95

By a certain age we must know that the causal sequences, or the chains of causation, that are initiated by insignificant events in our lives, by situations or actions that we might not even remember, can lead to what is significant and vital. At least we are probably dimly aware of something along that line. (Some people realize this even as children, but I'm talking about ordinary people.)

We have no way of knowing if a tiny twinge, or an indisposition that, never recurring, we forgot long ago, or an unweaned kitten we brought into the house, or a person we saw and took a liking to one summer's eve, with the result that we became lovers, could someday directly or indirectly contribute to our death or, even, suffice by itself to kill us. Once we find out, it is already too late. Contend and struggle though we may, it usually proves next to impossible to change the outcome.

Yet here and there we may get a chance to sever the causal chain, to break out of it or to stop and redirect what seemed to be inevitable. A remark, a question, or a delay—especially if gauged and tuned accurately—can change everything. Most of the time, though, we fluff the chance—sometimes owing to our overoptimism and sometimes to our oversubtlety—and we ourselves ordain our fate and unknowingly ratify it.

Couldn't these legs, this human trunk, these hands, this face—all that I kiss and kiss—be those of my murderer, my death, either now or long after this night, near this bed or far from it? Can't they? Won't they? What use will the clarity of hindsight have when it informs me of the connections I failed to make, or the things I failed to say or do? Except to show me that blindness and stupidity can grow in me as well as in others?

Plainly there is something else underneath all this. It is the latent desire to experience my death—for that matter, our deaths—at the hands of someone loved, that is, at the hands of a creature it is impossible to imagine shrinking from. This could lead us to still other conclusions.

But the important thing is something else. My basic feeling of insecurity, as an explanation, does not undo the factual linkage in events.

96

I have planned a nullification of N. This deaf kid, as we used to know him, who has been getting rid of everyone who once helped him should be annihilated in such a way that it will constitute a triumph for me.

When he killed Sevim, who had come to talk to him and warn him, he for the first time had in a way a rational justification for murder. Sevinç and I are next in line. But when my turn comes, I have a surprise in store for him.

He launched a game in which he played opposite all of us. At the beginning, none of us caught on. The rule he played by was to oppose all those around him and to give them, in turn, the chance to go against him. When his opponents entered into a dispute with him, they—at times—found it possible to persuade him without suppressing their personality and individuality. On the other hand, he set himself up as somebody to be fought against, provoking in his opponents reactions and sentiments against him. He was well aware that people soon tire of an authoritarian leader.

Besides, he enjoyed the game. His greatest gain was perhaps the boundless pleasure he derived from it. He created his opponents' reactions himself, and he knew it.

But there was more to the game. Shifting ground, N adapted his position in ways calculated to engage individual opponents, constantly changing who he was in the game of conflict. Although he maintained a core consistency, he was a different person in the eyes of each of his opponents—of each member of his circle—so that they could not agree about who or what they were discussing when they ventured to speak of him among themselves. They had to content themselves with disparaging one another's "mistaken" notions, views, and opinions.

97

FOOTNOTE (S). [Here, under this heading, there appeared no entry. Whoever wrote this seems to have anticipated that S (Sevinç? Probably) would be adding something. Yet, though I have been reading in a notebook, I have the feeling that the contents are nothing more than scribbles on scraps of paper, little more than doodling, that have been copied out into it. Everything seems put together at random . . . —A Reader]

[*Addendum:* In Chapter 93, some "found" papers are mentioned. These are also supposed to be worked into the notebook. Confusion and disorder now reign not only in the disposition of chapters but also at the level of paragraphs and lines. I think I am getting caught up in the atmosphere of these notebooks.]

98

It was getting dark. Even on foot, negotiating the potholes was becoming more difficult. Once again I had reached the end of a street. The Avenue of Gaps was far below me. There were only a few people walking along this avenue on which pedestrians and vehicles once flowed like a river, almost without interruption. One by one people vanished into doorways. The cars I could see were not parked in front of the houses or at the new dead ends of the side streets but were haphazardly positioned as if abandoned. Cars that no longer had anywhere to go.

Shutters in various styles—considered one of the hallmark architectural details of houses on and near the Avenue of Gaps ever since the older ones had been built—were being drawn shut, although in all my life I have rarely seen them shut, only in a few houses and then only for the months when the owners went to their summer places. When I heard that the hinges made no noise except for a thin and almost pleasant screech despite the dust and grime that must have settled on them over the years, I concluded that a lot of cleaning and oiling had taken place during the five days since I had last been in the neighborhood.

It was getting dark, and I was becoming worried. It was necessary to walk to the end of each street in order to see if it led anywhere and then to double back if it turned out to be a dead end. After that it was try another street, and then another. On my fourth try, a bit of sky stuck in the space between the old houses that lined the street I was on. That was the only spot around that held any light.

Full of apprehension, I quickly headed back toward the middle of the block, abandoning the attempt to reach the Avenue of Gaps. A door to my right had been left open. It was fitted with the sort of ornamentation popular seventy years ago, and the frosted glass behind its heavy iron framework was dully transparent under the dust. The fifteen-watt bulb illuminating the entrance went out. I just managed to get inside, and I went up one flight. A wood-and-ironwork door with glass panes was opened quietly. I entered. The door closed behind me. "It's lucky you made it," the woman said. "In a minute, the people on the street will begin to vanish. Take a seat and catch your breath . . ."

99

Steel. Plane tree. Mountain. Stone.

We long for solidity and find its paradigms in the domain of metals and the arboreal, in the durable forms of nature and in nature as shaped by man. In what man finds in the world and in what he can make. We have always considered man a weak, impotent, feeble creature. If that were not the case, would we admonish him to become as sturdy, as hardy, and as tough as this or that? Would we accept counsel like that or teach it? Man would seem to have confidence not so much in himself as in what he produces and creates from the resources at hand.

Sevinç no longer comes to see me. At times I ask myself if all that has happened was some strange dream. I say at times, because generally I find it hard to forget that I'm confined here. All that has happened, all that I have written and related, is no dream. At times I've told it as if it were a nightmare, and at times I've laid out the sober details. Does Sevinç exist or not? He has not been around lately, and he has not read what I have written.

I imagine that no one has so far guessed that I live far removed from the sounds of the world. At any rate, I don't talk with the maintenance crew that comes daily. The way I stare at their lips, not to miss anything they might say, puts them off a little, I'm afraid.

I was the power, the puppet master, behind the man who seemed to be running everything. I was responsible for making the decisions, setting the objectives, and coming up with the ideas and the words to be used. Few have a glimmer of what all this means. Most think that what is visible is all there is. The only ones who know what goes on behind the scene are those who hold the strings in their hands.

100

There were only a few places to rest. Someone got up and offered me his low stool. I sank onto it. I hadn't realized how exhausted I was.

I seemed to be in a bachelor's pad. But it appeared to be overflowing with people of both sexes. In the room I was ushered into, there were ten of us. Including the people going in and out of rooms, there were perhaps forty-five to fifty who had taken refuge here. What else can I say but refuge?

The idea I have of a bachelor's pad is of a place that, besides not being well appointed, verges on receiving no care at all—or looks that way—even if it is clean and orderly. No point in arguing now whether I have the right picture.

Anything a person could sit on had been lined up along a wall, and rolled and folded bedding had been piled in one corner. Some people sat cross-legged in the center; those who moved in and out walked around the edges of the room. In a little while, they sat me down on a trunk by the wall, in front of a collapsible outdoor table. I had nothing with me to eat, but most of the others seemed to have come prepared. A little bread and cheese satisfied me for the moment. Several men took off their shirts, hung them up, and put on pajama tops. All the bedding was spread out on the floor, with little space between. The bathroom became busy, and toothbrushes were wiped dry and put back into bags—handbags, briefcases, and bookbags. Some people retired to other rooms, while others came into the room where I was, obviously following rules settled before I arrived, which I couldn't make out. The young man who had shared his bread and cheese offered me half of his mattress. Our common lack of pajamas recalled something I could not quite reconstruct, but I didn't brood about it. The light was turned off. We stretched out, with no shyness about touching each other. "You really don't recognize me?" he whispered in my ear. I squeezed his wrist but hesitated to answer aloud. At that moment, a terrible screech of brakes came from someplace close by. There was running in the street. We heard a wild scream as of sudden internal pain—of bones breaking, for instance—and then there was silence. The people lying around the room stirred. Then, once more, a hush fell over us. Our hands definitely recognized each other. For some people desire has no end, unless they are very ill.

101

A day comes when we each understand we must free ourselves of the enchantment of words, we must give up yielding to the magic of words that are nothing more than clichés and sentimentalities. A day comes when we realize we must teach ourselves to speak, to feel, and to think in our own way, just as we learned to walk, to eat, and to evacuate in our own way. This is true for all of us. Sooner or later. The day our feelings, thoughts, and words truly become our own . . . The funny thing is that the moment we begin speaking like ourselves, many around us start to complain that they don't see rhyme or reason in what we say, that they find our prating bizarre and incomprehensible. There are fools who feel violated if they are addressed with anything but the forms they are used to. You almost wish on these poor souls the extremity that would wake them up.

The writer, however, by virtue of his role has to depend on forms that are accessible to everyone, as well as to forge a language of his own. The moment he begins to write, he becomes a creator of forms. Does his mastery, his acrobatic finesse, depend on braiding the two thin wires he must travel into one slightly more substantial tightrope? I'm well aware that in talking about the writer, I haven't defined exactly whom I mean. What I'm thinking of is a specific kind of writing and a specific kind of writer. Every word can be blown out of proportion. No one has as yet pierced the mystery of simple and precise speech. *Night* could have become an effective word without being inflated. A word with the power to make the animal inside us shiver.

102

This place, this moment—was it a dream or wasn't it? I could not say. A piece of purplish sky in the window was growing lighter. So I was awake. My companion prodded me slightly. "The sooner we get out of here, the better," he said. "It won't be pretty if they raid the place." People had a strange way of talking lately. Did everything I was hearing seem odd to me because we hadn't for quite some time been speaking as much as we had before? Perhaps the less one speaks, the more meaning—proper or improper—one loads on one's language.

We had hardly finished dressing when all the lights in the house came on. Those rushing in seemed to come in force. We pulled ourselves together. I found myself in the front row as the squad entered the room. The others, even those to the left and right of me, stood a little to the rear. The leader of the squad pulled up a chair, turned it around, and straddled it. The others lined up a step behind him. Counting the leader, there were eight of them. Since there were some forty-five of us, it wasn't a certainty that the intruders would get out alive. But it seemed better to wait for them to attack us before attacking them. As if those were the rules.

The man on the chair looked us over one by one.

The place was quiet. I seemed to be catching on, as if someone were whispering in my ear, or as if I were reading an invisible manual: for instance, spending the night in a "night shelter" like this was a criminal offense, as so much other behavior had come to be. Everyone was expected to arrange his excursions in a way that let him return home in time in the evening. Nobody was fooling anybody with the expedients employed to avoid vanishing: yes, more and more people were carrying pajamas, underwear, and toothbrushes around with them. Shelters like this one had appeared out of the blue in all the neighborhoods. But they were soon discovered and raided. People found in the shelters could not be made to disappear, for they had not been caught in the street. But there were ways of dealing with them too. The man on the chair was still looking us over. I heard someone behind me mutter under his breath, "Tie your shoelaces, mister, for God's sake. He's looking for an excuse." The man got up from the chair, and as he walked toward the corner, I caught sight of the person who had whispered to me. Practically a child. "Tie your shoelaces," he insisted. Doing so would have drawn attention. The man was already looking my way. "Have you noticed how many of us there are in this house?" I asked the youth, loudly enough that he could hear me without straining. "Forget the house, do you know how many are in this room?"

Of course, he knew.

103

"One of the words we must stop being enchanted by, perhaps among the most important, is the word *man*. We use the word as if it is a talisman, for voicing our loftiest sentiments. But we have no compunction about oppressing and destroying human beings individually—be they friend or foe—with the help of that edifying word. When it suits us, we make the word *man* our most powerful tool, our spear of aggression, loading it with a meaning imagined, projected, invented, desired.

"Let us stop placing man on a pinnacle, and let us stop living as if we believed that man is far more important than animals, plants, water, or mountains, that everything has been created in order to serve man. Then, perhaps, we'll understand the real worth of man—we'll give him the respect that is due him as something significant only together with animals, plants, water, mountains, and stones."

How strange! It was I who once wrote those words. I defended them. But after night closed in on us, I did my utmost to convince everyone that they were fatuous.

No one knows the value of sleep better than I do. Ever since I've been out of my teens, I haven't been able to sleep enough, to get a good sleep, except during a few brief periods when I lived as others wanted me to and not as I wished. And when I'm working, it's a constant battle to keep my eyes from closing and to keep myself from dozing off as I start to dream with my eyes open. I cannot tolerate noise when I'm working, but I've also had to bolt out of libraries and museums to escape the incapacitating sleepiness and oppressive fatigue their silence produces in me. My sleep is never sound at night. I want to sleep, yet I fear sleep. Even so, it no longer terrifies me that people are put to sleep through the use of tones, words, images, ideas, and incantations. Oh no, I no longer turn a hair.

104

If we all acted at the same time, we could devastate this squad. Anything I said that the boy behind me could hear easily I could be sure the squad and their leader—who, at any rate, was looking at me—would hear as well. Playing into my hands, the leader looked me right in the eye and snorted, "You say something?" Certain that a booming voice would carry more weight, I said without hesitation, as if eager to share my thoughts, "I was just wondering how many of us there are in this room. That was my question. I'd say it's a question that matters, considering that whether you get out of here alive hangs on it." Then, after counting one, two, three, I finished what I had to say: "By the time you managed to shoot us dead, we could throttle you with our bare hands."

Then I woke up. It was daybreak. I looked at my feet. I laughed. What will we be imagining next? What dreams, what fictions are we apt to construct? No matter what we do, the events around us outdistance by far what we're able to contrive in our dreams and fictions. Since we no longer give thought to those who are killed, lost, or beaten to a bloody pulp but instead feel an affinity with those who do the killing, the abducting, and the maiming, even our fantasies have become second-rate in comparison with the real-life exploits we know of. We no longer worry about resisting or about protecting and defending ourselves from killing, disappearance, and dispersal. Even when we dream of that sort of thing, we soon wake up.

Once more I've read my little parable. I like it. A few corrections may be needed here and there. I'll read everything again an hour from now, and if the corrections still seem necessary, I'll make them before sending the manuscript to the newspaper. The signature will be that of a famous writer, which I'll sign to the piece. The editors will want to print it, though they may be surprised that the fellow has changed his style so completely.

The publication of the piece under this writer's name, not to mention the public reaction to the account and the perplexity resulting from its publication, will bring people to ask questions. Maybe the newspaper will cut out parts before publishing it. That too is possible. On the evening of its publication, I'll have a small task left to take care of.

105

Sevinç isn't a real person. I made him up. In part, his words and actions are based on remembrance of a love far back in my past; for the rest, they are inspired by my sessions with the utter quack who tries to talk to me at this hospital where I've been held for months. When I told him I would no longer show him my notebooks, he didn't insist. Sevinç died then—I should perhaps say, at that very hour. Sevim isn't a real person either. And perhaps there is no one who calls his assistant Sevim. Most probably not. A woman who was killed? . . . I cannot say. I'm in no position to state categorically that there was no such woman. For many people are killed, or are forced to kill themselves, or are made to suffer pain, on and off the record. That much is true. More accurately, I should say that that much must be true.

Something astonishes me. People talk about how killing, tormenting, and harassing are terrible. Is it possible that they have never come up against someone who persecutes, or attempts to persecute, them? Is there no one on whom they would like to avenge themselves? Have they never met someone who will not take their hand when they extend it, who will not accept what they have to offer, who will spurn it? Have they never felt the impulse to use every means necessary to get others to accept their ideas? How can they not desire to imprint the order lying in their hearts and minds onto the world as if with a stamp? Don't they realize that the only way to succeed at that is to kill, if necessary, or if, for whatever reason, killing is precluded, to torment and harry? To deceive and to lie? How can they not understand?

How far can it go? Until no one remains but yourself. Until you see only yourself in any mirror. Until other people's eyes become your mirrors. Or rather, until all the mirrors reflect you even though you are not standing in front of them. Until people's eyes are good only for reflecting the fear you inspire in them, even if you are not in their hearts. Is not everything in this world ultimately what is seen, imagined, or thought by whoever tells of it—by the person who makes it possible for others to assimilate it, that solitary person, that single intelligence? Does not everything boil down to that?

Even if we do manage to deceive everyone else, even if deception is the nub of what we do, should we not refrain from deceiving ourselves?

106

The small task that remains is this: throwing the newspaper down on the boardroom table and then, without so much as requesting the floor, questioning the president's committee, "Are we to allow this?"

Then the wheels will roll on their own.

In my opinion, the most crucial of our schemes is the final one, I should say my own. The groundwork has been laid with care over the past three weeks. The principle of it is this: those for whom adverse fortune might be expected must not meet with any misfortune, or in other words, those on whom misfortune is visited must not have been—themselves or their closest friends—in any position to predict it. The well-known writer, for example, will make almost no headway in getting people to believe that he didn't write the piece published under his name, and more crucially, he will know that even if his readers accept his denials, we will not. He has no way out! He will not even be able to confide in his associates, for he won't be sure that no one among them will use his confidence to do him harm. Of my many accomplishments, this is the one I am most proud of. No one trusts anyone anymore. While the writer is still rubbing his temples in confusion, it will be up to my men to forestall the accident that the committee will have devised to befall him an hour or two after its meeting; my men will have to gun down those who are going after him. When our writer, unaware of what almost happened to him, returns home, slides in the bolt, prepared to spend a night filled with anxiety, those in the back alley who have crushed the faces of four dead bodies beyond recognition will shoot and kill, say, the seventh person who walks across the intersection after a certain hour. After dragging the body a little farther into the alley, they will perhaps stick a gun into its hand and melt into the night. The functionary who reports this to me will be the only person to have seen me, and he will be leaving for distant parts within a few days. In any case, he will never be seen again. Not a costly method, when all is said and done. Provided that the third man who is to die, or the seventh, or the tenth, is not someone whose death could have been expected.

107

My father was becoming insistent. For days I had been doing most of my reading in my hideaway. He could see I was hiding something, since I usually read out in the open. He wanted to take a look at the book. I tried to put him off, piled excuse upon explanation, but I was no good at lying. My father seized the knob and forced the door open. My elbow went into the middle of the full-length mirror on the door. Instantly, three large cracks radiated from that spot all the way to the frame. Without the least show of concern for my elbow, my father stalked off. My elbow was all right. As it turned out, he did not take a look at the book. The book remained in my hideaway. I was not given my weekly allowance for two years. It took that long to replace the mirror. I had turned fifteen by then. I couldn't make friends with the new mirror: it showed me as a single person whereas for two years there had been three of me, however distorted.

Something is coming to an end. I am sitting at my window, studying the leaves on the trees. None of them are identical. Each is different. Human beings' eyes, hands, mouths, bodies are all different. Certain people have to be eliminated. But which ones? Or the ones in which mirrors?

I have written that I planned a nullification of N. But N has disintegrated on his own. His illness no longer leads to anything of value; instead, it harms him. The balance is off. It must be put right again.

He keeps making inquiries, it seems, about who is behind everything. I am determined to show him, I swear. If I were he, instead of killing off the characters I "created," whether based on real persons or entirely fabricated, I'd consider it more reasonable to kill off the person of "the writer." What ways could a writer find or imagine to finish off his persona? That is, if he hadn't gone off the rails as he has now.

Perhaps something like this . . .

108

Paris. The Metro. Its smell, defying description, is unforgettable once inhaled. You miss it later. In a few seconds, as the train emerges from the darkness, someone will push me. I am staring at the dark mouth of the tunnel. I must not look around me. I must not see the person who pushes me.

The train arrives. I board it. Nobody pushes me. I keep insisting. It's no use.

109

I get shoved through a doorway. Into pitch-darkness. Perhaps it won't help to wait for my eyes to become accustomed to the dark, for in this darkness there is not a drop or a speck of light. I do not know why, but I slowly begin walking almost heel to toe, one foot in front of the other, compelled toward somewhere or other, as if someone has prodded me slightly. I go on walking like this for what seems a very long time. Then, all of a sudden, I think I've gone blind. Yet, a few seconds later, I realize that my eyes are dazzled, that somewhere ahead, far off, or above, there is a very powerful light. As He shoved me in, He said, "Now you get what you want." From ahead, in the distance, I see a familiar face approach. A familiar face that I cannot place. I am in agony at not being able to recognize it, to connect it with anything, to place it. When the face gets much closer, for a moment I think it resembles His; then I change my mind. As it gets even closer, the face looks more like the woman called Sevim, although in a masculine guise. Then I recognize the face. I know it belongs to Sevinç, and I realize that it has all been a trick my dazzled eyes have played on me. Sevinç looks at me, smiling slightly mockingly. I have a sudden urge to strangle him. I make for his throat like a madman. In dreadful pain, as if being slashed in every part of my body, I hit the ground amid a terrifying crash. Next to the shattered light, He, Sevinç, Sevim, and a deaf blond kid are all laughing at me as if they were all one face, covered with blood, looking back at me perhaps in the mirrors, or on the floor, or in my mind. A viscous pain is all over me, and that very old, thick scent. As the light slowly dims, at last I am myself, reflected in every fragment. The self that I did not recognize in the mirror. Thousands of fragments. Hundreds of thousands of fragments that are no longer me at all.

B**** K*****
April, 1975–September, 1976

110

Can writing all this keep one from going mad?